The gun is like a tumor on my thigh as I walk through the morning streets against the wind that never dies down. April sunlight stings my eyes but the wind dissipates its heat, blustering against store windows and kicking debris into the gutters.

At Ninth and Spruce, I pause and look up at the three-decker and the windows of the second floor, where Larry LaSalle can be found at last. Does he suspect my presence here on the street? Does he have a premonition that he has only a few minutes left to live?

I am calm. My heartbeat is normal. What's one more death after the others in the villages and fields of France? The innocent faces of the two young Germans appear in my mind. But Larry LaSalle is not innocent.

HEROES

A novel by

ROBERT CORMIER

Published by
Dell Laurel-Leaf
an imprint of
Random House Children's Books
a division of Random House, Inc.
1540 Broadway
New York, New York 10036

Visit us on the Web! www.randomhouse.com/teens

Educators and librarians, for a variety of teaching tools, visit us at www.randomhouse.com/teachers

ISBN 0-440-22769-0

RL: 5.7

Reprinted by arrangement with Delacorte Press

Printed in the United States of America

February 2000

20 19 18 17 16 15 14

OPM

To George Nicholson and Craig Virden
With thanks

Show me a hero and I will
write you a tragedy.

F. Scott Fitzgerald

My name is Francis Joseph Cassavant and I have just returned to Frenchtown in Monument and the war is over and I have no face.

Oh, I have eyes because I can see and eardrums because I can hear but no ears to speak of, just bits of dangling flesh. But that's fine, like Dr. Abrams says, because it's sight and hearing that count and I was not handsome to begin with. He was joking, of course. He was always trying to make me laugh.

If anything bothers me, it's my nose. Or rather, the absence of my nose. My nostrils are like two small caves and they sometimes get blocked and I have to breathe through my mouth. This dries up my throat and makes it hard for me to swallow. I also become hoarse and cough a lot. My teeth are gone but my jaw is intact and my gums are firm, which makes it possible for me to wear dentures. In the past few weeks, my gums began to shrink, however, and the dentures have become loose and they click when I talk and slip around inside my mouth.

I have no eyebrows, but eyebrows are minor, really. I do have cheeks. Sort of. I mean, the skin that forms my cheeks was grafted from my thighs and has taken a long time to heal. My thighs sting when my pants rub against them. Dr. Abrams says that all my skin will heal in time and my cheeks will someday be as smooth as a baby's arse. That's the way he pronounced it: arse. In the meantime, he said, don't expect anybody to select you for a dance when it's Girls' Choice at the canteen.

Don't take him wrong, please.

He has a great sense of humor and has been try-ing to get me to develop one.

I have been trying to do just that.

But not having much success.

•   •   •

I wear a scarf that covers the lower part of my face. The scarf is white and silk like the aviators wore in their airplanes during the First World War over the battlefields and trenches of Europe. I like to think that it flows behind me in the wind when I walk but I guess it doesn't.

There's a Red Sox cap on my head and I tilt the cap forward so that the visor keeps the upper part of my face in shadow. I walk with my head down as if I have lost money on the sidewalk and am looking for it.

I keep a bandage on the space where my nose used to be. The bandage reaches the back of my head and is kept in place with a safety pin.

There are problems, of course.

My nose, or I should say my caves, run a lot. I don't know why this should happen and even the doctors can't figure it out but it's like I have a cold that never goes away. The bandage gets wet and I have to change it often and it's hard closing the safety pin at the back of my head.

I am wearing my old army fatigue jacket.

So, I am well covered up, face and body, although I don't know what I am going to do when summer comes and the weather gets hot. Right now, it's March, cold and rainy, and I will worry about summer when it gets here and if I am still around.

Anyway, this gives you an idea of what I look like when I walk down the street. People glance at me in surprise and look away quickly or cross the street when they see me coming.

I don't blame them.

• • •

I have plenty of money.

I received all this back pay when I was discharged from Fort Delta. The back pay accumulated during the time I spent in battle in France, and then in the hospitals, first in France, then in England.

My money is in cash. Hundred-dollar bills and twenties and tens. The smaller bills I keep in my wallet but the rest of the money is stashed in my duffel bag, which is always with me, slung over my shoulder. I am like the Hunchback of Notre Dame, my face like a gargoyle and the duffel bag like a lump on my back.

I am staying in the attic tenement in Mrs. Belander's three-decker on Fourth Street. She finally answered the door after I had been knocking for a while, and regarded me with suspicion, not recognizing me. This was the proof that the scarf and the bandage were working in two ways: not only to hide the ugliness of what used to be my face but to hide my identity.

As her small black eyes inspected me from head to toe, I said: "Hello, Mrs. Belander." A further test.

She didn't respond to my greeting and I realized that she didn't recognize my voice, either. My larynx, which Dr. Abrams called my organ of voice, had also been damaged by the grenade and although I can speak, my voice is much lower now and hoarse, as if I have a permanent sore throat.

I remembered what Enrico Rucelli in the last hospital had said about how money talks and I began to draw out my wallet when she said:

"Veteran?"

I nodded, and her face softened:

"Poor boy."

I followed her up the four flights of stairs, the blue veins in her legs bulging like worms beneath her skin.

The tenement is small, with low slanted ceilings. Two rooms, kitchen and bedroom. The bed, only a cot, really. But everything very neat, windows sparkling, the floor gleaming with wax, the black stove shining with polish.

I glanced out the kitchen window at the steeples of St. Jude's Church. Craning my neck, I caught a glimpse, between the three-deckers of the neighborhood, of the slanted roof of the Wreck Center. I thought of Nicole Renard, realizing I had not thought of her for, oh, maybe two hours.

I turned to find Mrs. Belander with her hand out, pink palm turned upward.

"In advance," she said.

She was always generous when I did her errands, and her tips paid for my ten-cent movie tickets at the Plymouth on Saturday afternoons. She baked me a cake for my thirteenth birthday. That was five years ago and it seems like a very long time. Anyway, I paid her a month's rent and she wrote out a receipt on the kitchen table. The table was covered with a red-and-white-checkered oilcloth like the ones we had at home until the bad times arrived. My caves moistened and I groped for my handkerchief.

She handed me the receipt. It read *Tenant* in her shaky handwriting where my name should have been.

That was fine with me. At that moment I knew that I was really anonymous, that I wasn't Francis Joseph Cassavant anymore but a tenant in Frenchtown.

"Thank you, Mrs. Belander." Testing again.

"You know my name," she said, responding this time. Not a question but a statement, suspicion returning to her eyes.

I thought quickly.

"On the mailbox downstairs," I answered, guessing that her name was there. But a good guess, as she nodded, satisfied.

"Stop later, my place," she said, her Canadian accent making the words sing. "I make you sturdy soup to help your cold . . ."

After she left, I went to the window and looked at the falling rain outside. I was home again in Frenchtown. I thought of the gun hidden away in my duffel bag, and knew that my mission was about to begin.

• • •

Later, I light a candle in St. Jude's Church.

The smell of burning wax and the fragrance of old incense—the odors of forgiveness—fill the church. I remember the days I served as an altar boy for Father Balthazar and the Latin responses I had trouble memorizing.

I kneel at the communion rail and say my prayers.

I pray for Enrico and hope that he will finally go home and adjust to his condition, although those are terrible words: *adjust* and *condition*. Enrico is now without his legs and is also missing his left arm. "Thank Christ I'm right-handed," he once said, but I don't think he was really thanking Christ.

I also pray for the souls of my mother and father.

My mother died when I was six, giving birth to my brother, Raymond, who lived only five and a half hours. My father died five years ago of a heart attack in the rub room of the Monument Comb Shop, although I always felt he really died with my mother all those years before. I offer up prayers, too, for my uncle Louis, who gave me a place to live until I joined the army.

I pray, of course, for Nicole Renard, wherever she may be.

And finally, I pray for Larry LaSalle.

It's hard for me to pray for him and I always hesitate before I can bring myself to say that prayer. Then I think again of what Sister Gertrude taught us in the third grade, words that she said came from the mouth of Jesus. Pray for your enemies, for those who have done you harm. It is easy to pray for those you love, she said. But it counts more to pray for those who don't love you, that you don't love.

So I offer up an Our Father and Hail Mary and Glory Be for Larry LaSalle. Then I am filled with guilt and shame, knowing that I have just prayed for the man I am going to kill.

• • •

Before going to bed, I stand in front of the mirror in the bathroom.

My hair is a mess as usual, thin in some spots,

thick in others. For some reason, my hair began to fall out in clumps my first few days in the hospital in France and it has grown back the same way.

I apply Vaseline to my cheeks.

I make myself look at my caves and the way the shape of my mouth has changed because of the dentures. I roll the dentures around in my mouth and remember what Dr. Abrams said, that I should have a better-fitting pair made in a few months when my gums stop shrinking. He also gave me his address in Kansas City, where he will be in practice when he returns from the war. "Great strides have been made in cosmetic surgery, Francis," he said. "One of the few benefits of the war. Look me up when you've a mind to." He was tall and looked like Abraham Lincoln. And should practice his cosmetic surgery on himself, Enrico said.

Enrico always had something to say. About anything and everything. I sometimes think that he talked so much to cover up the pain. Even when he laughed, making a sound like a saw going through wood, you could see the pain flashing in his eyes.

"If you want to forget Nicole," he said one afternoon when we were tired of cards and checkers, "here's what you do." He put down the deck of cards he was practicing on, to shuffle with one hand. "You get out of the army and get yourself to a home for the blind. There must be a good-looking blind girl somewhere just waiting for a nice guy like you."

I looked to see if he was joking. Even when he was joking, though, it was hard to tell because his voice was always sharp and bitter and the pain never left his eyes.

"You're a big hero," he said. "A Silver Star hero. You should have no trouble finding a girl as long as she can't see your face." He tried to shake a cigarette from his pack of Luckies and three or four fell to the floor. "A blind girl, now, is right up your alley . . ."

I am not a hero, of course, and I turned away in disgust but later that night, lying awake, I wondered if I could really find a blind girl to love me. Ridiculous. What made me think that a blind girl would automatically fall in love with just anyone at all?

"Forget it," I said to Enrico the next day.

"Forget what?" His voice was a gasp from the pain in his legs, which were not there anymore. He kept massaging the air that occupied the space his legs used to fill.

"About the blind girl."

"What blind girl?"

"Never mind," I said, closing my eyes against the sight of his hand clawing the air.

"It's still Nicole, isn't it?" he said.

I did not have to answer because we both knew it was true.

It would always be Nicole Renard.

And even though I am home from the war, I wonder if I will ever see her again.

I saw Nicole Renard for the first time in the seventh grade at St. Jude's Parochial School during arithmetic. Sister Mathilde was standing at the blackboard illustrating a problem in decimals when the piece of chalk in her hands broke and fell to the floor.

I leaped to my feet to retrieve the chalk. We were always eager to keep in the good graces of the nuns, who could be ruthless with punishments, using the ruler like a weapon, and ruthless, too, with marks on our report cards.

As I knelt on the floor, the door opened and Mother Margaret, the Sister Superior, swept into the classroom, followed by the most beautiful girl I had ever seen.

"This is Nicole Renard. She is a new student here, all the way from Albany, New York."

Nicole Renard was small and slender, with shining black hair that fell to her shoulders. The pale purity of her face reminded me of the statue of St. Thérèse in the niche next to Father Balthazar's confessional in St. Jude's Church. As she looked modestly down at the floor, our eyes met and a flash of recognition passed between us, as if we had known each other before. Something else flashed in her eyes, too, a hint of mischief as if she were telling me we were going to have good times together. Then, the flash was gone and she was St. Thérèse once more, and I knelt there like a knight at her feet, her sword having touched my shoulder. I silently pledged her my love and loyalty forever.

Sister Mathilde directed her to a vacant seat in the second row nearest the window. She settled herself in place and didn't give me another glance for the rest of the day.

After that first meeting of our eyes Nicole Renard ignored me, although I was always aware of her presence in the classroom or the corridor or the schoolyard. I found it hard to glance at her, both hoping and fearing she'd return my glance and leave me blushing and wordless. She never did. Was the look that passed between us that first day a wish of my imagination?

Luckily, she became friendly with Marie LaCroix, who lived above my family on the third floor of our house on Fifth Street. The girls often walked home from school together—Nicole lived one street over on Sixth—and I trailed after them, happy to be following in Nicole's footsteps. They giggled and laughed, their schoolbooks pressed against their chests, and I hoped that one of Nicole's books would fall to the ground so that I could rush forward and pick it up.

Once in a while Nicole visited Marie on the third floor, and I lurked on the piazza below, trying to listen to their conversations, hoping to hear my name. I heard only the murmur of their voices and occasional bursts of laughter.

Standing at the banister in an agony of love and longing, like a sentry on lonely guard duty, I waited for Nicole to come down the stairs so that I could get a glimpse of her and perhaps catch her attention. She'd come into view, my mouth would instantly dry up, and I would look away, afraid that my voice would emerge as a humiliating squeak if I tried to say hello. A moment later, I'd hear her footsteps fading away and I'd plunge into an agony of regret, vowing to talk to her the next time.

Often, in the evening, when families gathered on the piazzas, the men drinking beer they had brewed in big crocks in the dirt-floored cellars and the women mending socks and knitting as they chatted, I'd seek out Marie and try to get her to mention Nicole Renard. Although we were separated by that chasm of being twelve years old, when boys and girls barely acknowledged each other's existence, Marie and I spoke to each other once in a while because we lived in the same three-decker.

Sitting on the steps, we'd talk about everything and nothing. She liked to tell jokes. She'd imitate Sister Mathilde, who had trouble with her digestion and tried to disguise her burps behind her hand, and sometimes rushed out of the classroom, slamming the door behind her. "She lets off her farts in the corridor," Marie maintained, doing a quick imitation of those corridor farts.

Baseball was a big topic with us. Monument has always been a baseball town, and Frenchtown teams, made up of players from the shops, often won the city championship in the Twilight Industrial League. Marie's older brother, Vincent, was an all-star shortstop for the Frenchtown Tigers, and my father, whose nickname was Lefty, had been an all-star catcher for the same team years before.

I kept wondering how to bring Nicole Renard into the conversation. She had no brothers and sisters about whom I could inquire. I didn't know whether she liked to read or who her favorite movie stars might be. Finally, I plunged. We had fallen into a comfortable silence, listening to the men arguing mildly about the Red Sox, and I said: "Nicole Renard seems very nice." Feeling the color creeping into my cheeks.

Marie turned and fixed her eyes on me.

"Yes," she said.

I said nothing more. Marie didn't speak, either. My father's voice reached us with his old refrain: how selling Babe Ruth to the Yankees had brought a curse upon the team.

"Do you like her?" she asked finally.

My breath came fast. "Who?"

An exasperated sigh escaped her. "Nicole, Nicole Renard."

"I don't know," I said, cheeks incinerating now. I didn't know what to do with my hands.

"Then why did you ask about her?"

"I don't know," I said again, feeling stupid and trapped, knowing I had fallen into Marie LaCroix's clutches and that she'd probably blackmail me forever.

Finally, I threw myself on her mercy. "Yes," I said. "I like her." Astonished at the relief I felt at this admission, I wanted to shout from the rooftops: "I love her with all my heart."

"Please don't tell her," I pleaded.

"Your secret is safe with me," Marie said.

But was it? Yet deep within me was the knowledge that I wanted her to tell Nicole Renard that I loved her.

Three days later, Marie and Nicole again passed time together on the piazza above mine. I sat reading *The Sun Also Rises*, realizing that Ernest Hemingway seldom used big three-syllable words, which made me wonder if anyone, including me, could become a writer.

When I heard Nicole making noises of departure, her footsteps crossing the floor as she called "Bye-bye" to Marie, I closed the book and perched on the banister, positioning myself where it would be impossible for her to ignore my presence.

Hearing her footsteps on the stairs, I curled my legs around the rungs of the banister.

She came into view.

I didn't look away this time.

"Don't fall off, Francis," she said as she passed quickly by and went down the stairs.

I was so startled by her voice, by the fact that she had actually spoken to me, that I almost did fall off the banister. Regaining my balance, I realized that she had actually spoken my name. *Don't fall off, Francis.* My name had been on her lips! Then I winced in an agony of embarrassment. Why hadn't I answered her? Did she now think I was stupid, unable to start a conversation? Had she merely been teasing me? Or had she been really afraid that I might fall off the banister? The questions left me dazed with wonder. I never knew that love could be so agonizing. Finally, the big question: Had Marie told Nicole that I liked her?

I never learned the answers to those questions. Marie and I never talked about Nicole again. She was always coming and going in a hurry, and I was too timid to try to corner her. Summer vacation started and everyone fell into different routines. Nicole didn't visit our three-decker anymore. I caught sight of her sometimes on Third Street going in or coming out of a store, and my breath held. I saw her strolling the convent grounds with Sister Mathilde one hot summer afternoon.

One evening as I hung out in front of Laurier's Drug Store with Joey LeBlanc and some other kids, I saw her walking across the street, her white dress a blur in the darkening evening. She looked our way and waved.

I waved back, thrilled at her attention.

Joey also waved, calling out: "Hey, Nicole,

you've got a run in your stocking." Laughing at what he thought was a witty remark. He couldn't see her stockings at that distance, of course.

Nicole paused, tilting her head as if puzzled; Joey burst into more laughter, and Nicole walked on, quickening her step.

"You've got a big mouth," I told Joey, turning away in disgust.

"What's the matter with you?" he asked.

I didn't answer.

I wondered whether she'd been waving at Joey LeBlanc or me.

I feel like a spy in disguise as I walk the streets of Frenchtown, hidden behind the scarf and the bandage, making my way through the chilled morning, pausing on the corners, watching the people come and go, and then moving on when I feel their eyes on me filled with either pity or curiosity.

I try to avoid eye contact with people I know, like Mr. Molnier, the butcher, who stands in the doorway of his meat market in his bloodstained apron, and Mrs. St. Pierre, who scowls her disapproval at him as she passes.

I have places to visit now that I have returned and one of them is Sixth Street and the gray three-decker where Nicole Renard lived with her mother and father on the second floor at number 212.

I know she doesn't live there anymore and I have nothing to gain by going there but it's inevitable that I look at her house again.

I stand across the street for a long time, staring up at the blank windows with their white lace curtains.

After a while, a child's small face appears at a window on the second floor, like the ghost of the little girl Nicole once was. I smile up at the child and she draws away from the window, disappearing the way Nicole disappeared from Frenchtown. Or was the child a momentary hallucination?

Crossing the street, I climb the steps to the first-floor piazza and look at the nameplates beside the black mailboxes. Langevin, Morrisette, Tourigny. The Morrisette nameplate shines with newness and has taken the place of Renard. I stare at the final proof that Nicole has gone away.

I don't know where they went, the Renards. They left without warning, in the middle of the night.

That's what Norman Rocheleau told me in a village outside Rouen one evening. His outfit came through the village we were occupying temporarily, and we recognized each other from across the street. He was older by three years but we had both gone to St. Jude's Parochial School and we talked about Sister Perpetua in the sixth grade, who was notorious with the ruler. Extend your palm, she'd order for the slightest infraction, and the ruler descended almost mechanically.

Norman and I made a swap, my ration of Chesterfields, which I did not smoke anyway, for his military edition of *The Great Gatsby*, which I'd heard was a great novel. We continued to talk about the old days in Frenchtown as we drank *vin rouge* like the heroes in a Hemingway novel, sitting on the steps of a bombed-out farmhouse.

As twilight softened the ragged edges of the broken houses, and the wine began to lower my defenses, I got up the courage to ask him:

"Hear anything about the Renards?" Almost afraid to say her name.

He said it for me: "Nicole!" Then: "Didn't you go out with her for a while?"

Hearing her name aloud on the evening air in a foreign country, I was unable to find my voice.

"Yes, she was my girl," I said finally, giving in to a rush of memories: our lips meeting, her hand in mine as we walked down Mechanic Street, the cologne like spring flowers that always clung to her.

Dragging on the cigarette and releasing the smoke through his mouth and nostrils, he told me about the family's sudden departure from Frenchtown. More than that:

"All kinds of rumors about her, Francis. She began to stay at home, didn't come out of the house except for the five-thirty morning mass, the nuns' mass, which nobody else in his right mind ever goes to. She was like . . ."

He gestured with the cigarette, trying to find the right word. ". . . a hermit. Then she was gone. Her and her family. Left Frenchtown without telling anybody." Gazing at me curiously: "Haven't you heard from her?"

"No," I answered.

He squinted at me, curiosity remaining in his eyes. "You're about fifteen, right? How did you get in the army?"

I told him about forging my birth certificate. He didn't ask why I joined and I didn't expect him to. Everyone wanted to go to war in those days to defeat the Japs and the Germans.

After a while, we fell into a tired, end-of-a-long-day silence. Then he left to rejoin his outfit, walking off into the twilight. He turned and we saluted each other in a half-joking way, grinning, because we didn't think of ourselves as soldiers but only as two Frenchtown boys in uniform.

And I had not yet killed anybody.

• • •

As I turn to go back down the steps at 212 Sixth Street, the front door swings open to reveal a woman in a damp apron, a broom in her hand, looking at me with narrow suspicious eyes.

"You want something?" she asks.

I wonder if she is using the broom as a weapon for protection and don't blame her. I have to keep reminding myself how I look to other people.

"Do you know where the Renards went?" Not expecting an answer but hoping that the question provides me with respectability.

"What?" she asks, frowning as she clutches the broom in front of her.

The scarf has muffled my voice, of course.

"The Renards," I say, trying to pronounce the words distinctly. "Where are they?"

"All gone," she says, her voice doleful. "All gone."

She begins sweeping the doorstep as if she intends to sweep me away, too.

Her words chase me down the steps and into the street: *All gone, all gone.*

• • •

Mrs. Belander is waiting when I return from Third Street, two bags of groceries from Henault's Market in my arms. I have stocked up on cocoa and bread and strawberry jam, and a variety of Campbell's soups in the red-and-white cans, mostly tomato and bean and pea soup. Everything soft because my gums are tender and it's hard for me to chew. I have also bought two bottles of pasteurized milk, a pound of butter and a wedge of cheddar cheese, which I will store in the small electric refrigerator on the counter upstairs. I can keep going on a minimum of food because I lost my appetite somewhere in France and eat now only to sustain myself for a while.

Mrs. Belander holds a deep pot in her hands and says: "I will carry it up for you, the black bean soup I made."

We climb the stairs together.

In the tenement, I place the groceries on the counter and she puts the pot on the stove. "No boil," she says. "Just heat . . ."

Then turns to me. "You didn't say your name." Not quite an accusation but as if her feelings have been hurt.

Here is the point where my life becomes a lie.

"Raymond," I tell her, using the name of my dead brother. "Beaumont," I add. My mother's name before she married my father.

"Père et mère?" she asks.

I am ready to give those answers. "In Canada." In my mind, I substitute heaven for Canada. "We lived in Boston before but they went back home to Canada when the war came." The truth is that my uncle Louis, who never became a citizen, returned to Canada while I was in the army.

I see the question in her eyes and am quick to answer:

"I met a Frenchtown boy in the service. Norman Rocheleau. He told me about Frenchtown. He made it sound like a nice place to live."

Doubt flashes in her eyes and I make a quick addition to my story.

"My mother and father are waiting for me in Canada. But I have to report to Fort Delta for treatments for a while."

It scares me, how easy it is to lie.

"Vous parlez français?" she asks.

I shake my head no. I can understand French because of the eight years with the sisters at St. Jude's but have never been able to speak the language correctly.

She sighs heavily, studies my scarf and bandage for a long moment and murmurs "Poor boy" again as she shuffles toward the door.

• • •

The tenement is heated only by the black stove in the kitchen, fed by a glass oil jug that I will have to fill every day or two from the big metal barrel in the backyard. The stove throws heat only into a small area of the kitchen, and the rest of the tenement is damp with cold even though winter has gone.

I make myself a cup of cocoa, stalling, delaying the moment of going to bed, despite the cold. The clock on the wall, in the shape of a banjo, tells me it is twenty-five minutes after eleven, which means that a long night stretches ahead. I yearn for sleep, my eyes raw and burning, but I know that the dreams will begin when I close my eyes and drift off.

In the bathroom, I apply more Vaseline to my cheeks.

Finally, I slip into bed. Mrs. Belander has provided me with extra blankets and I pull them up to my chin. I double the pillow under my head to prevent the phlegm from running down my throat, causing me to choke and cough.

• • •

I can never trace the moment when I finally fall asleep, that blurred line between wakefulness and oblivion. While waiting, I silently recite the names of the guys in my platoon—Richards and Eisenberg and Chambers and, yes, Smith—and their first names or nicknames—Eddie and Erwin and Blinky and Jack. Then, more last names, Johnson and Orlandi and Reilly and O'Brien and *their* first names, Henry and Sonny and Spooks and Billy—and then start all over again, arranging them this time in alphabetical order, still waiting for sleep to come.

I don't want to think about them, those GIs in my platoon. I don't want to recite their names. I want to forget what happened there in France but every night the recitation begins, like a litany, the names of the GIs like beads on a rosary. I close my eyes and see them advancing in scattered groups through the abandoned village, ruined homes and debris-cluttered streets, our rifles ready, late-afternoon shadows obscuring the windows and doorways and the alley entrances. We are all tense and nervous and scared because the last village seemed peaceful and vacant until sudden gunfire from snipers erupted from those windows and doorways and cut down the advance patrol just ahead of our platoon. Now I can hear Henry Johnson's ragged breathing and Blinky Chambers whistling between his teeth, the village too still, too quiet. "Jesus," Sonny Orlandi mutters. Jesus: meaning *I'm scared*, and so is everybody else, clenched fists holding firearms, quiet curses floating on the air, grunts and hisses and farts, not like the war movies at the

Plymouth, nobody displaying heroics or bravado. We are probably taking the final steps of our lives in this village whose name we don't even know and other villages are waiting ahead of us and Eddie Richards asks of nobody in particular: "What the hell are we doing here, anyway?" And he's clutching his stomach because he has had diarrhea for three days, carrying the stink with him all that time so that everybody has been avoiding his presence. Now gunfire erupts and at the same time artillery shells—theirs or ours?—boom in the air and explode around us. We run for cover, scrambling and scurrying, hitting the dirt, trying to become part of the buildings themselves but not safe anywhere.

I find myself in a narrow alley, groping through rising dust, and two German soldiers in white uniforms appear like grim ghosts, rifles coming up, but my automatic is too quick and the head of one of the soldiers explodes like a ripe tomato and the other cries *Mama* as my gunfire cuts him in half, both halves of him tumbling to the ground.

I explode into wakefulness along with the booming artillery and I find myself gasping, instantly wide-eyed, not cold for once in Mrs. Belander's tenement, the sweat warm on my flesh, but in a minute the sweat turns icy. In the alley that day I encountered the German soldiers, all right, but my bursts of gunfire killed the soldiers quickly, no exploding head, no body cut in two, although one of them did cry *Mama* as he fell. When I looked down at them, in one of those eerie pauses that happens in an attack—a sudden silence that's even more terrible than exploding shells—I saw how young they were, boys with apple cheeks, too young to shave. Like me.

"Hey, Francis, come on," yells Eddie Richards and I join him in a scramble out of the alley and into the woods, his smell still heavy in the air, and we stumble around in the woods until nighttime, when we run across the remains of our platoon and learn that Jack Smith and Billy O'Brien are dead and Henry Johnson wounded, his chest ripped open by shrapnel, carried off somewhere behind the lines and we never see him again.

The next day, the grenade blows my face away.

• • ••

The morning sun slashes my eyelids and I blink at daylight spilling through the window. I have survived another night, endured the dreams and the memories again although I'm not sure anymore which are the dreams and which are the memories.

My limbs are stiff and the raw places of my flesh sting but I grope from the bed, coughing, my throat filled with phlegm.

Ignore it all, I tell myself, and count your blessings.

You're back in Frenchtown and your body is functioning. You have a nice dry place to stay and a mission to perform.

And maybe this will be the day that Larry LaSalle will appear on the streets of Frenchtown and you will be able to carry out that mission.

I tell myself that I will not visit the Wreck Center, that there is nothing to gain by going there just as the visit to Nicole's house on Sixth Street brought back only loneliness and regret.

Yet even as I acknowledge the futility of such visits, I am walking in the direction of the Wreck Center at the far end of Third Street, bending against the never-ending March wind.

Then a hand grips my shoulder, stopping me in my tracks, and a voice whispers in my ear:

"Land mine?"

Turning, raising my eyes under the visor of the Red Sox cap, I find Arthur Rivier looking at me curiously. The curiosity is softened with sympathy.

I shake my head, not deserving his sympathy.

"Grenade, then?" he asks.

My silence provides him with his answer and he murmurs: "Tough . . . tough . . ."

His eyes are bleary and bloodshot and there's no recognition of me in them, for which I am grateful.

Before he enlisted in the army, Arthur Rivier had been a star first baseman for the Frenchtown Tigers and hit booming home runs over the fence at Cartier's Field. I remember when he returned on furlough in his khaki uniform with the corporal's stripes, along with the other servicemen home temporarily from the war. I wanted to be like them, these heroes, fighting the Japs and the Germans, going off to battles on land and sea. I was impatient to reach the age when I could join them in that great crusade for freedom.

Arthur Rivier points to the entrance of the St. Jude Club and says: "Come on, I'll buy you a drink . . ."

The club is where the young men of Frenchtown gather to shoot pool and play poker and drink beer and wine and hold Saturday-night dances for their girlfriends after a long week in the comb and button shops. The rules require a member to be twenty-one years old before joining and every Frenchtown boy looks forward to that birthday.

At my hesitation, Arthur says: "You deserve a good drink . . ."

Inside, the club is crowded and smoke-filled, billiard balls clicking and everyone talking at once and a sudden blast of music from the jukebox, "Don't Sit Under the Apple Tree with Anyone Else but Me," which I last heard on a radio in the English hospital.

Familiar faces turn toward me. Big Boy Burgeron and Armand Telliere and Joe LaFontaine and some others, all of them veterans and survivors, ballplayers and shop workers who became fighting men in uniform.

"Beer," I answer, raising my voice above the din when Arthur asks me what I want to drink. I drank beer for the first time in the English hospital when Enrico bribed a male nurse on the late shift to bring us a few bottles. The beer was warm and bitter but at least a change from all the medicine I had to swallow every day.

I gulp the beer now, lifting the scarf, as Arthur enters into a discussion with Big Boy Burgeron about whether it would be better to become cops or firemen now that the war is over.

Big Boy, who weighed about three hundred pounds before entering the service and is now sleek and hard with no soft edges, says firemen offer the best career because you don't have to march or walk as a fireman. "With my luck, as a cop I'd end up walking a beat. And I'm not walking anymore—the infantry spoiled my feet . . ."

"I could never climb a ladder," says Armand Telliere, speaking to nobody in particular as he lines up a shot at the pool table. "Besides, they say cops will be riding in cars on patrol from now on. Walking or riding, no more piecework at the shop for me . . ."

"College for me," Joe LaFontaine announces, holding up his beer and studying the way light strikes the glass. "The GI Bill. The government's willing to pay, so I'm going . . ."

"You didn't even graduate from high school," Arthur Rivier says but in a joking way, laughing. Others join in the laughter, creating a camaraderie in a bar, a fellowship that I wish I could be a part of.

"I can make up the studies," Joe LaFontaine replies. "They're going all out for veterans." He takes a swift gulp of the beer. "I'm going to college," he proclaims, raising his voice so that everyone can hear. "I'm going to be a teacher."

"Sister Martha must be turning over in her grave," Armand Telliere says.

"That would be a trick," Arthur says. "I saw her just last week. Still knocking guys around in the eighth grade. No bigger than a peanut and she still knocks them around."

"The way she knocked you." Big Boy laughs.

And everybody joins in the laughter, and someone calls for another round and the jukebox plays "I'll Be with You in Apple Blossom Time," such sweet voices in the air.

Arthur turns to me. "You don't talk much, do you?" he says.

I want to ask about Larry LaSalle, if anyone knows when and if he's coming back, but I don't want to call more attention to myself. The scarf and bandage are enough to cause curiosity.

"That's all right," he says, "you earned the right not to talk."

What if I told him that I was little Francis Cassavant who shagged balls behind the bases when the Frenchtown Tigers played their crosstown rivals, the West Side Knights, for the Monument championship? That I am not the hero he thinks I am, not like the other veterans here in the St. Jude Club.

As the big argument resumes about cops and

firemen, I slip out of the bar unnoticed, into the March dampness of Third Street. I make my way through the throng of shoppers and the schoolkids leaving St. Jude's school, my identity protected by the scarf and the bandage. My head is light from the beer because I haven't eaten since my breakfast, when I forced myself to drink the coffee and eat the oatmeal.

I am on my way, of course, to the Wreck Center.

The Wreck Center is boarded up and abandoned now, the words FRENCHTOWN REC. CENTER faded and barely visible above the front door. The door's red paint has turned a faint sickly pink. My caves begin to run and my scarf is damp and, after a moment, I realize that it's not the moisture from my caves that has dampened my scarf.

It's a bad-luck place, people had said.

A place of doom, others added.

In the old days it had been known as Grenier's Hall, and the children of Frenchtown, myself among them, often heard its tragic story.

Not a tragic story at the beginning, however. The hall had been a place of happy events—gala dances and fancy balls to mark occasions like New Year's Eve and the Fourth of July. It became a traditional place for wedding receptions, the bridal party marching the length of Third Street to the hall after the wedding mass at St. Jude's.

Until the wedding of Marie-Blanche Touraine.

Marie-Blanche married a handsome Irisher by the name of Dennis O'Brien from the plains of North Monument after breaking off her engagement to Hervey Rochelle, the shipping room foreman at the Monument Comb Shop. At the reception, during a pause between the dinner and the dancing, as Marie-Blanche and Dennis cut the wedding cake, Hervey burst into the hall, a gun blazing in his hands. A moment later, Marie-Blanche lay bloody and dying in her wedding gown. A bullet entered Dennis O'Brien's spine, leaving him paralyzed for the rest of his life. Hervey hung himself that evening in the toolshed behind the comb shop.

That was the end of Grenier's Hall as a festive gathering place. The doors were sealed and the windows shuttered. Children shivered as they listened to the story of that day of doom, and always hurried by the abandoned building. Some claimed that on windy nights when the moon was full, the sounds of moaning and weeping could be heard if you pressed your ear against the front door. It became a Frenchtown tradition for children to listen at the door at midnight on the night of a full moon as a rite of passage. Before my turn arrived, however, Grenier's Hall was given a reprieve and began a new existence.

I was in the seventh grade, the year that Nicole Renard came into my life, when the hall's transformation began. People rushed to the site one Saturday morning as word spread through the streets that carpenters and painters were attacking the building in a frenzy of activity. I rushed to the scene and watched in amazement as trucks and vans, emblazoned with the words CITY OF MONUMENT, disgorged teams of workmen who, we learned, had been hired under a new municipal program. In the next few days the men worked frantically, scraping and painting, replacing doors and windows, tarring the roof. But the work was haphazard. Workers dropped hammers, spilled paint, stumbled over each other and occasionally pulled brown paper bags from their pockets and took quick gulps from hidden bottles.

"It's like watching a Marx Brothers movie," said

Eugene Rouleau, the barber whose tongue was as sharp as his razor.

When the workers finally completed the job, the building still looked unfinished. The white paint didn't completely cover the dark patches of mildew on the clapboards and the shutters sagged next to the windows.

"Look," someone called.

As we watched, the sign that read FRENCHTOWN REC. CENTER slid from its place above the front entrance until it hung at a drunken angle above the door.

"It's still a bad-luck place," Albert Laurier of Laurier's Drug Store said.

People nodded in agreement, remembering the wedding reception of Marie-Blanche Touraine.

That night, someone crossed out the words on the sign and replaced them with WRECK CENTER in bright red paint. Although the sign was restored to its original wording, the place was known ever since as the Wreck Center to the people of Frenchtown.

The center opened its doors the day after St. Jude's Parochial School closed for summer vacation. I stood with the other kids at nine o'clock on that June morning in front of the building. A tall slim man stepped into view, a lock of blond hair tumbling over his forehead, his smile revealing dazzling movie-star teeth.

"Good morning," he said. "My name is Larry LaSalle."

"Is that his real name?" Joey LeBlanc asked in a whisper that carried over the crowd. He was often punished by the nuns for talking out of turn.

"That's right—it's real," Larry LaSalle said. And for some reason, the crowd applauded.

Larry LaSalle had the broad shoulders of an athlete and the narrow hips of a dancer. He was both. He swung the bat with authority as he hit home runs in games at the sandlot next door and later led us through vigorous exercises and calisthenics. He was also a dancer, with a touch of Fred Astaire in his walk, his feet barely touching the floor. He could tap-dance with machine-gun speed and make daring leaps across the stage. But he was most of all a teacher, leading classes in dancing, arts and crafts, organizing a choral group, directing musical shows.

The Wreck Center became my headquarters in the seventh and eighth grades, a place away from the sidewalks and empty lots of Frenchtown. I had never been a hero in such places, too short and uncoordinated for baseball and too timid to join the gangs that hung around the street corners.

I had no best friend, although Joey LeBlanc, who lived on the first floor of my three-decker, often went with me to the Plymouth on Saturday afternoons. He kept up a steady commentary during the movie, like a radio announcer describing the action. He didn't like to read and I loved roaming the stacks of the Monument Public Library, where I discovered Ernest Hemingway and F. Scott Fitzgerald and Jack London and rushed home with an armful of books.

Home was the tenement where I lived with my uncle Louis, my father's brother, a silent giant of a man who was a yardman at the Monument Comb Shop. He took me in after my father died, cooked our meals and cleaned the apartment. He drank three bottles of beer every night while listening to the radio, volume turned low, until his bedtime at eleven o'clock. He seldom spoke but I never doubted his affection. He patted me on the head, passing by as I read my books at the kitchen table, and listened solemnly as I told him of my day at school, a duty he required every night at supper. "You're a good boy, Francis," he'd tell me as he handed over my fifty-cent allowance every Friday night.

The loneliness of the tenement drove me to the Wreck Center after school and on weekends. Without talent for singing or dancing or arts and crafts, I finally joined calisthenics after Larry LaSalle made a speech urging everyone to participate in at least one activity. I picked a spot in the back row to avoid calling attention to myself, and Larry LaSalle didn't embarrass me by calling me to the front row where the shorter kids belonged.

Larry LaSalle was everywhere in the center, showing how strips of leather could be made into key chains, old wine jugs into lamps, lumps of clay into ashtrays. He tamed the notorious schoolyard bully, Butch Bartoneau, convincing him that he could sing, coaching him patiently day after day, until Butch's version of "The Dying Cowboy" brought tears to the eyes of everyone in the Wreck Center's first musical production, *Autumn Leaves*.

"But he still beats up kids in the schoolyard," Joey LeBlanc observed.

Under Larry LaSalle's guidance, Edna Beauchene, tall and gawky and shy, became the hit of the show, dressed like a bum and dancing an intricate routine with ash cans, winning applause like a Broadway star.

"You are all stars," Larry LaSalle always told us.

Rumors told us that Larry LaSalle had also been a star, performing in nightclubs in New York and Chicago. Someone brought in a faded newspaper clipping showing him in a tuxedo, standing beside a nightclub placard that read STARRING LARRY LASALLE. We knew little about him, however, and he discouraged questions. We knew that he was born in Frenchtown and his family had left to seek their fortunes elsewhere. Larry had taken dance lessons at Madame Toussaint's studio downtown as a boy and had won first prize in an amateur contest at Monument City Hall when he was nine or ten.

Why did he turn his back on show business and return to Frenchtown?

No one dared to ask him, although there were dark hints that he had "gotten into trouble" in New York City, a rumor Joey LeBlanc delighted in repeating with raised eyebrows and a knowing look.

Dazzled by his talent and his energy, most of us didn't dwell on the rumors. In fact, the air of mystery that surrounded him added to his glamour. He was our champion, and we were happy to be in his presence.

Nicole Renard began coming to the center that first winter and joined the dancing group. She had taken lessons in Albany and instantly caught the attention of Larry LaSalle. I'd watch her glide across the floor, catching flashes of her white thighs as she twisted and turned. She seemed to exist in a world of her own, like a rare specimen, birdlike and graceful as she danced, separate from the rest of the dancers. She didn't join any of the classes or do exercises or crafts and would simply leave when the dance classes were over.

One day as she headed for the exit, drops of perspiration on her forehead like raindrops on white porcelain, she said:

"Hello, Francis."

That same strange teasing in her voice that I'd heard when she'd warned me about falling off the banister. I gulped, coughed, managed to utter "Hello" but was unable to bring her name to my lips.

She paused, as if to say more, our eyes meeting in the same connection I had felt in Sister Mathilde's classroom. A moment later, she was gone, leaving behind a sweet fragrance mixed with the musky smell of her perspiration, and the after-image of her body leaping through the air. She didn't remind me of St. Thérèse anymore but of the girls in certain magazines at Laurier's Drug Store who set my heart racing and made my knees liquid.

Nicole Renard's visits to the Wreck Center made my life there complete.

That's why Joey LeBlanc angered me when he said he could feel that old doom hanging over the place.

"You talk too much," I said, slamming the door behind me as we left the center one afternoon.

"Doom," he pronounced. "Wait and see."

• • •

Shivering now as the rain begins to fall, I turn away from the Wreck Center, knowing that poor Joey LeBlanc, who died on a beach on Iwo Jima in the South Pacific, had been right, after all.

I have been in Frenchtown almost a month now, and March has turned into April but the clouds are still thick and low, and rain falls almost every day. I walk the streets and people begin to nod at me or greet me with a smile because I have become a familiar figure. My army fatigue jacket tells them I am a veteran and this is a season when all the veterans are welcome everywhere.

Lingering in front of stores, standing on the front steps of St. Jude's Church at the corner of Third and Mechanic, I watch for Larry LaSalle, for that Fred Astaire strut and that movie-star smile. I think of the gun in my duffel bag and I'm impatient for him to come back.

I sometimes stand in front of the convent and wonder whether the mystery of what has happened to Nicole is hidden within those walls.

The veterans in the St. Jude Club always greet me with big hellos and slaps on the back and make room for me at the bar or in the crowd watching a close game of pool. They respect my silence and my anonymity. The talk now is of the new Chevies and Fords coming from the Detroit factories and the freedom of walking down Third Street without saluting an officer and wearing civvies instead of the uniform.

Arthur and Armand and Joe are always there, fixtures in the club until they become cops or firemen or go to college or back to the shops but this is the pause between one life and another and they drink beer and wine, and shoot pool and talk, always the talk, reminiscing about the days before the war, the nuns at St. Jude's, the long sermons of Father Balthazar, the ball games in Cartier's Field and the mystery of the stranger visiting Frenchtown one summer years ago who hit a home run in almost every game and who many thought was a major-league player in disguise. Babe Ruth, maybe. Or Lou Gehrig.

I let my glass of beer grow stale and flat on the bar because I want to remain sharp and alert at all times in case Larry LaSalle should walk in or someone might mention his name.

The Old Strangler lets me nurse my beer and doesn't mind if I don't order another. He is the bartender, the sweeper and the settler of arguments. Arthur says he used to wrestle in the carnivals that came to Frenchtown, taking on the traveling champion who challenged local wrestlers. He was famous for his stranglehold, which paralyzed his opponents. His voice is hoarse from the time, Arthur says, that he was hit in the Adam's apple by a carnival champ who was losing the match. His hair is sparse and gray but his eyes are clear and watchful and his muscles bulge under the white shirt, his bow tie moving when he talks.

There always comes a moment when a sudden quiet falls in the club, as if everyone has become weary and yet it's too early to go home. The jukebox, too, is silent. I watch and see things. I see the twitching in the corner of Arthur's mouth, the way his lips seem tugged by invisible fingers. Armand stares off into space, looking at something nobody else can see, and there's a sudden flash of . . . what?—terror? bad dreams?—in his eyes. As I turn away, I see George Richelieu tugging at his pinned-up sleeve, which should hold his arm but his arm is buried somewhere in the South Pacific or probably tossed aside into jungle growth, as Arthur muttered one day. In the deepening silence I hear my own voice, loud in my ears, as I break the mood with the question that has been burning inside me since my arrival in Frenchtown:

"Has anybody heard when Larry LaSalle's coming back?"

My voice surprises me, suddenly strong and clear, without the hoarseness. Arthur's eyes are upon me, curious and suspicious. He studies me for a moment, then turns away, raising his glass:

"To Larry LaSalle," he calls out, "the patron saint of the Wreck Center."

I wonder if he is making a joke or being sarcastic but he nods meaningfully at me, holding his glass high.

"And to the kids who were lucky to know him," adds Joe LaFontaine, raising his own glass.

Everyone joins in and I am surprised to see the Old Strangler pour himself a glass of red wine. I have never seen him drink before.

"To the Silver Star and the men who wear it,"

he growls. "And to Larry LaSalle, the best of the best . . ."

"Hey, Strangler, still got the scrapbook?" Arthur asks.

The Strangler sets down his glass, reaches under the bar and pulls out a big black leather book. Glancing at me, he says: "They're all in here." The cover reads FRENCHTOWN WARRIORS in white block letters. He riffles through pages of newspaper clippings and pictures of men and women, all in uniform.

He holds the scrapbook up at a double page, with headlines, articles and pictures of Larry LaSalle. The biggest headline at the top of one page proclaims: LT. LASALLE EARNS SILVER STAR.

"There are lots of medals," the big bartender croaks, "for outstanding service, but only the Silver Star is for heroism." His old voice is suddenly formal and dignified. "For gallantry."

Another headline halfway down the page reads:
LASALLE CAPTURES ENEMY,

SAVES FELLOW MARINES

"The dancer becomes a hero," Arthur says. Then pauses and turns to me. Leaning close, he says: "That voice when you asked about Larry LaSalle. Now I know it. You're Francis Cassavant." Final recognition in his eyes. "You used to—"

"Shag balls during the games at Cartier's Field,"

I say, voice low, afraid that my days of being anonymous are over.

His eyes widen, and he declares: "You have your own Silver Star. You're in the Strangler's book, too."

As he turns to announce my identity, I touch his shoulder. "Don't make a fuss, Arthur. Let me stay like this." Indicating the scarf and the bandage.

"You deserve to be recognized, Francis," he whispers. "You're a goddamn hero." Shaking his head in disbelief. "Little Francis Cassavant. Falls on a grenade and saves—how many men did you save, Francis? How many men were you willing to die for?"

Lifting the scarf, I sip the beer, doing something to avoid answering his question.

A long moment passes. "Okay, you have my respect. If you don't want to talk about it, I won't either." Slapping me on the back. I look away from the admiration in his eyes. "And I'll keep your secret."

The Strangler places the book back under the counter and he swipes at the top of the bar with a damp rag.

"It's good that I don't have to keep adding to the book anymore," he says. Then looking at me and answering my question: "Nobody knows when he's coming back. But they all come back to Frenchtown sooner or later."

Arthur nudges me. Still whispering, he says: "The Wreck Center. Ping-Pong! You were the champ there at Ping-Pong, right?"

"Table tennis," I correct him.

I correct him gently, remembering Larry LaSalle and my brief moment as the table tennis champion at the Wreck Center.

What's the matter?" Larry LaSalle asked.

"Nothing," I replied.

He found me sitting alone on the back steps of the Wreck Center, looking at nothing in particular. There was nothing in my world that was worth looking at. Inside, the chorus was rehearsing for the *Follies and Fancies* production, singing "Happy Days Are Here Again," the words like a mockery in my ears. I was aware of other kids busy at the craft tables.

"It must be something," Larry LaSalle said, dropping onto the step beside me.

"I'm rotten at everything," I confessed. "I can't sing. I can't dance. I'm no good at baseball." And I can't even get up the nerve to hold a normal conversation with Nicole Renard, I added silently.

Avoiding his eyes, I was suddenly angry at my self-pity. Snap out of it, I told myself.

"I've been watching you, Francis. During calisthenics. You have outstanding reflexes. You have a natural athletic gait." He spelled out the word. "*G-a-i-t*. I think I have the perfect sport for you."

In spite of my doubts, my interest quickened. Larry LaSalle's opinion could never be dismissed.

"Look, today is Tuesday. The center's closed for renovations for a couple of days to bring in new equipment. Be here Friday afternoon. You're going to be a champion."

"I'll be here," I promised. Where else would I be?

When I arrived at the center three days later, I was surprised to see that the place had been entirely rearranged. A small stage had been built at the far end of the hall and two spotlights installed. "For the musical shows," he explained. A vending machine stood near the entrance. Two Ping-Pong tables occupied spaces near the side windows, looking out on Third Street.

Leading me to the nearest table, he picked up the white plastic ball and bounced it a few times.

"Ping-Pong," I said, hoping my voice didn't betray my disappointment.

"Table tennis," he said. "Ping-Pong is a game, table tennis is a sport. Known around the world. It's a sport you're going to dominate with your quickness and your reflexes."

Pointing to two paddles on the table, he said: "Let's get going."

He showed me how to stand: alert, leaning forward, knees bent slightly, paddle in my right hand, level with my belt. Going to the opposite side of the table, he hit the ball to me. I swung the paddle, struck the ball with a satisfying *plop*, and watched it sail cleanly over the net. The ball returned. I hit it again. Bounce on his side and return to mine. Bounce and return again. Suddenly the ball arrived, but squirted crazily to my right. Instantly alert, I reached, managed to hit it with the paddle, saw it fly just as crazily across the net.

"Beautiful," Larry LaSalle called. "You returned the spin."

We played for almost an hour, as kids gathered to watch this new sport. Sweat pasted my shirt to my body and glued the racket to my hand. I missed some shots, particularly the balls with spin, which made them go wildly askew, but returned most of them. The crowd often cheered Larry LaSalle and once or twice a cheer went up when I made a lunging return.

Nobody had ever cheered me before.

Finally, he threw down the paddle, called a halt, and led me to the new vending machine, where he bought me a Coke. "Congratulations, Francis," he said, raising his bottle in a toast. "You're a natural. Besides the reflexes, you have what I call sweet anticipation. It's what natural athletes have, anticipating where the ball will land, whether it's baseball, football or table tennis."

I stood spellbound by his words.

"You also have a great return. That's the key, Francis. Let the other players make the moves, put on the spin, kill the ball. You just keep returning it, good and steady. Your opponent will get frustrated, careless, make a mistake." He gulped down his Coke in one long swallow. "Tomorrow I'll teach you the chop on defense and the spin on offense."

Just as he had lured awkward girls into ballet classes and ballplayers and bullies into being singers and dancers, so did he bring a sudden importance to table tennis. He gave lessons tirelessly, arranged contests, encouraged girls to take up the sport.

I spent hours at the tables, playing game after game, sharpening my chops and spins but focusing mostly on returns, trying to stay loose, flowing with the ball. My opponents often became frustrated as Larry LaSalle had predicted, their faces turning scarlet with anger while I stayed calm and composed, waiting for a mistake to be made. I didn't develop a spectacular kill shot like Joey LeBlanc. My spins were not as sharp as those of Louis Arabelle, who played with a smoothness that was deceptive: He stroked the balls almost lazily but they took unpredictable trajectories, never landing where they were expected. Yet I won my share of games and sometimes rang up a string of victories.

I often searched for Nicole among the spectators, especially if I was having a fine game. But she was seldom present. One afternoon, as I defeated Joey LeBlanc with five successive points that left him speechless for once, I turned to find her eyes on me. She brought her hand to her lips and flung it away. Astonished, I wondered: Did she actually blow me a kiss? Impossible. Or was it? The paddle slipped from my hand and dropped to the table. When I looked up again, she was gone.

• • •

In the dance classes, Nicole was the most talented of all, her slender body dipping and turning without effort, as if her bones were elastic. Jealousy streaked through me as Larry LaSalle tossed her in the air, letting her fly, defying gravity for a breathless moment, then caught her, pressing her close, their faces almost touching, their lips only an inch or so from a kiss before he allowed her to slip down against his body. He applauded her, his eyes looking deeply into hers, as she lay at his feet.

For the December production, he built an entire number around her and a song called "Dancing in the Dark." She glided in and out of shadows as the music played on a phonograph, and Larry LaSalle manipulated a spotlight he had installed especially for her performance.

He continued to give me extra lessons at the table, and we played countless games against each other. His eyes shone with admiration when I made an unusual shot. "My ambition for you, Francis," he said, "is to have you beat me." But he always won, with an array of attacks and returns that seemed effortless but always found their mark.

As the first weekend of December approached, excitement ran high through the Wreck Center when Larry LaSalle announced a "doubleheader"—a table tennis tournament on Saturday to be followed by the musical show *Follies and Fancies* on Sunday.

"Nicole's the star on Sunday and I want you to be the star on Saturday," Larry LaSalle said. "I'm not supposed to play favorites, Francis, but you and Nicole are special to me." I wondered if he suspected my secret love for her.

When I arrived at the Wreck Center on Saturday, kids had gathered around a silver trophy shaped like a player poised to serve the ball. I pictured Nicole handing me the trophy while I accepted it with the modesty of a true champion.

I was not scheduled to play until the afternoon through an elaborate system Larry LaSalle had devised to allow the ordinary players to eliminate themselves. The better players, like Louis Arabelle, Joey LeBlanc and me, were reserved to take on the morning's winners.

As the center echoed with the sound of bouncing balls and the whoops and applause of the spectators, I became restless and nervous. Suppose my spins and chops deserted me? What if my returns veered off the table?

Staring out the window, I sensed a presence nearby, a sudden disturbance in the air, and at the same time the drift of a delicate scent that I associated with Nicole Renard.

"Good luck, Francis."

I turned to find her there.

Speechless as always in her company, I managed a stupid smile.

"I love to watch you dance." I blurted out the words, surprising myself with my ability to say such a thing.

"And I love to watch you play," she said.

"You do?" Disbelief cracked my voice.

"You play table tennis like a dancer dances. The way you move. The way you hit the ball. Sometimes I hum a song, watching you play. It's like you're dancing to that song."

For the first time in my life, a tide of confidence swept through me.

"I'm having a party after the show tomorrow afternoon at my house. Larry says that's what people in show business do. Will you come, Francis?"

Her words filled me with both delight and agony, delight at her invitation and the instant agony of jealousy, the way she had casually said his name—not Larry LaSalle or Mr. LaSalle, as all the kids referred to him, but Larry, spoken offhand as if they were more than teacher and pupil.

Our conversation was interrupted by the announcement that the semifinal contests were about to begin. Nicole touched my shoulder, her hand both tender and caressing, and my flesh burned with the echo of her touch. "Good luck," she said.

Two hours later, I had survived more games than I could count, time passing in a blur as the ball zoomed back and forth across the table. Serve and return. Spin and chop. The kill shot, and the soft shot. My opponents went down in rapid succession. Finally, Joey LeBlanc, who was having a bad day with his serves, lost by a wide margin, 21–12, and went off muttering to himself.

Never before had I known such a sense of destiny. I felt invincible, impossible to defeat, the ball always under my control. The spectators often cheered, gasped at a spectacular shot, either by me or by an opponent, and fell silent when the outcome of a contest seemed in doubt. But I knew no doubt. Between games, my eyes sought Nicole and often spotted her, smiling encouragement. The center seemed vacant when I looked and did not see her.

Louis Arabelle also had been winning contest after contest at the other table, drawing his own cheers and applause. We glanced at each other between games and exchanged grins. It seemed inevitable that we would meet in the final contest of the day. Each time I heard a burst of applause for the next table, I knew that Louis had scored another spectacular point.

Finally, Louis and me. Standing across the table from each other. Both of us undefeated. Louis tall and rangy with long arms and legs, ready to play his deceptive game, never tense, never hurrying. I prepared myself for his soft strokes and dizzying spins and chops.

Louis took five quick points with his first round of serves, catching me off balance with the casual way he raised his paddle and the ferocity of the ball as it arrowed over the net toward me. A hush fell over the crowd.

I didn't panic, told myself to relax: This was a day in which I could not lose. My own five serves sent the game into a tie and after that I simply planted myself six feet from the table and concentrated on the return. Louis lost three points in a row and for the first time I saw him flushed with frustration, trying harder, frowning, and finally, making mistakes.

I reached twenty-one points to his eighteen by simply playing the game Larry LaSalle had taught me: being patient, remaining cool and composed while Louis pressed harder. As he missed his last remaining shot, which gave me the victory, a shout went up from the crowd, followed by cheers and whistles and the stomping of feet.

I turned, flushed with triumph, my heart beating furiously, blood pumping joyously in my veins. I saw Larry LaSalle coming through the crowd holding the trophy high above his head, saw Nicole beside him, her eyes on me, shining for me.

Like a dream coming true, Nicole took the trophy from Larry LaSalle and handed it to me, the radiance of her face mirroring my own.

The crowd grew silent as I pressed the trophy to my chest, my eyes becoming moist. Was I expected to make a speech?

"Better watch out, Mister LaSalle," Joey LeBlanc called out. "Francis has got your number."

Cheers and applause greeted his words and I wished I could find a way of gagging Joey LeBlanc and keeping his mouth shut.

Then a cry rose from the crowd:

"La-ree . . . La-ree . . ."

Calling him by his first name, finding the courage to do together what no one would do alone.

"La-ree . . . La-ree . . ."

Cringing inside, my moment of triumph tarnished and trashed. I knew they wanted Larry LaSalle and me to play for the real championship of the Wreck Center.

Then:

"Fran-cis . . . Fran-cis . . ."

More applause, shouts and whistles.

And a voice from the crowd:

"You can do it, Francis . . ."

Larry LaSalle inclined his head toward me, his shoulders raised in resignation, as if to say: It's up to you, Francis, how can we say no to the crowd and disappoint them?

Suddenly I thought: Maybe I can beat him. My play during the afternoon had been almost flawless;

even the game with Louis Arabelle, who was the best of them all, had been an easy win. Like the gamblers in the casinos who go on a winning streak, impossible to lose. Maybe I was on that kind of streak.

I nodded toward Larry LaSalle and picked up my paddle. Glanced again at Nicole and saw her smile of approval. Planted my feet firmly on the floor and took a practice swing.

A roar went up from the crowd.

The game began.

My serve.

Paddle met ball. I didn't try for speed or spin, merely wanted to place the ball in proper position, without risk, and then play my defensive game. My heartbeat was steady, my body poised for action. The ball came back to me. I returned. Came again, and again I returned. Larry LaSalle's return was placed perfectly, at the edge of the table, almost impossible for me to reach but somehow I reached it, returned it, throwing him off balance. My point. Next point his, then mine again. Then his.

We were halfway through the game, the score standing at 13–12, my serve, when I realized that he was letting me win, was guiding the game with such skill that no one but me realized what he was doing. He cleverly missed my returns by what seemed like thousandths of an inch, feigning frustration, and placed his returns in seemingly impossible spots but within my reach.

The noise of the crowd receded, diminished to a hush, broken only by the plopping of the ball on the table, the soft clunk of the ball on the rubber dimples of our paddles. A giant sigh rose from the crowd when an impressive point was made. I dared not take my eyes away from the game to look at Nicole.

Two games were being played at the same time, the sharp, take-no-prisoners game the hushed audience was observing and the subtle, tender game in which Larry LaSalle was letting me win.

Finally, the score stood at 20–19. My favor. One point away from victory. I resisted meeting Larry LaSalle's eyes. It was still his serve. Crouching, waiting, I finally looked at him, saw his narrowed eyes. They were suddenly inscrutable, mysterious. A shudder made me tremble as I realized that he could easily win the next two points and take the championship away from me. He could win it so easily and so humiliatingly that the crowd—Nicole—would know instantly that he had been toying with me all along.

The perfect serve came my way but my return was perfect. We entered a seesaw cycle, hit and return, repeating endlessly, near misses and lunging stabs, until finally the ball came to my side, a breathtaking shot that veered to the table's edge, causing the crowd to gasp, although he and I knew that it was within my reach. His final gift to me. Lunging, I returned the ball to the only place it could go, impossible for him to return.

He led the cheers, the hollers and whistles of celebration. Dashing to my side of the table, he pumped my hand, hugged me furiously, his ear close enough for me to whisper: "Thank you." He turned me over to the crowd as the cheers continued, my name endlessly shouted. My eyes sought Nicole, found her joyous face, hands joined together as if in prayer, eyes half closed as if making herself an offering to me.

A moment later, as the crowd broke up, she was suddenly in front of me, radiant, clasping my hand, whispering: "My champion." And leaning so close that her breath was warm on my cheek: "See you tomorrow."

But tomorrow was December 7, 1941.

Arthur Rivier is slumped against the brick building at the entrance of Pee Alley, and I know instantly that he is drunk. The streetlight catches his open mouth and the dribbles of saliva on his lips and chin.

Almost midnight and Third Street deserted. Restless in the tenement, I decided to walk the streets, telling myself that it was possible for Larry LaSalle to show up in Frenchtown at night as well as during the day.

Arthur Rivier blinks as he sees me approaching. "You okay?" I ask, even though I know he is not okay.

He regards me with bloodshot eyes, his lips turned downward like the mask of tragedy high above the stage at the Plymouth.

"Nobody talks about the war," he mutters, trying to focus his eyes and finally finding the focus and now his eyes drill into mine, the bleariness gone. "They talk about GI bills and going to college and getting married and joining the cops or the firemen but they don't talk about the war . . ."

I place my arm around his shoulder to support him as his body threatens to slide down the wall, a ridiculous gesture because he outweights me by at least fifty pounds.

He lifts his head to the night. "I want to talk about it, my war," he cries. "And your war, too, Francis. Everybody's war. The war nobody wants to talk about . . ."

"What war is that?" I ask, having to say something, having to respond to the sorrow in his voice. But not expecting an answer.

"The scared war," he says, closing his eyes. "God, but I was scared, Francis. I messed my pants. One day, running across an open field, so scared I shit my pants, bullets at my feet and everything let go . . ." Opening his eyes, he asks: "Weren't you scared?"

I remember the village and our advancing platoon and Eddie Richards saying: "What arc wc doing here, anyway?" And the smell of diarrhea.

"Everybody was scared," I tell him.

"Heroes," he scoffs, his voice sharp and bitter, all signs of drunkenness gone. "We weren't heroes. The Strangler and his scrapbook. No heroes in that scrapbook, Francis. Only us, the boys of Frenchtown. Scared and homesick and cramps in the stomach and vomit. Nothing glamorous like the write-ups in the papers or the newsreels. We weren't heroes. We were only there . . ."

Closing his eyes, he again slumps against the wall, as if the words he has spoken have used up all his energy.

Shadows loom in the alley's entrance and I look up to see Armand and Joe silhouetted against the lights of Third Street.

"Poor Arthur," Armand murmurs, coming forward, placing his arm around him, touching his face lightly. A deep snore flares Arthur's nostrils, flutters his lips.

Poor all of us, I think as I watch them lurching away with Arthur Rivier between them. A cold wind buffets the buildings and sends me hurrying back to Mrs. Belander's tenement.

Larry LaSalle was one of the first Frenchtown men to enlist in the armed services, announcing his intention on Monday afternoon, a few hours after President Roosevelt's address on the radio declared that a state of war existed between Japan and the United States, following the Japanese attack on Pearl Harbor. Patriotic fever, mixed with rage over the sneak attack in the Pacific, ran rampant through the streets of Frenchtown and, according to radios and newspapers, throughout the nation. Recruiting offices were immediately thronged with men and women answering the call to fight for their country.

Larry LaSalle stood before us that afternoon at the Wreck Center, the movie-star smile gone, replaced by grim-faced determination. "We can't let the Japs get away with this," he said, anger that we had never seen before flashing in his eyes. As we were about to cheer his announcement, he held up his hand. "None of that, kids. I'm just doing what millions of others are doing."

Larry's action became for us the beginning of wartime in Frenchtown. Other enlistments followed as fathers and brothers joined the armed forces. People gathered daily in Monument Square to say goodbye to the men being carried by buses to Fort Delta to enlist in the army and air force, and by train to the headquarters of the marines and navy in Boston.

The Frenchtown factories went on twenty-four-hour schedules as they began to manufacture material for the war effort. "We don't make guns and bombs," Uncle Louis said at supper one night. "But our men need everyday things—combs and brushes, buttons, knives and forks—life goes on, even in the service."

I had heard rumors that the Monument Comb

Shop, where Uncle Louis worked, was producing secret material in a special section of the factory. He lifted a gnarled finger to his lips. "Shhh," he said. A thrill went through me—a wartime secret in Frenchtown! Should we be on the lookout for spies?

Larry LaSalle's enlistment caused the Wreck Center to close for what people now called "the duration." The kids of Frenchtown hung out in St. Jude's schoolyard or in front of Laurier's Drug Store. Within a short time, the absence of young men on the Frenchtown streets was noticeable. At the Sunday masses, Father Balthazar prayed from the pulpit for the safety of our men and women in the service. Women, too, had begun to show up in uniform. They were called Waves and SPARS and walked the streets with a pride in their steps that hadn't been there when they were shop girls in the factories.

Young people and women took over some of the jobs in stores and factories. Mr. Laurier hired me to work part-time, after school and on weekends, at his drugstore. I ran errands, swept the floors, took out the rubbish and filled the shelves with stock from the back room. My special pleasure was stocking the candy cases with Tootsie Rolls, Butterscotch Bits and the big five-cent candy bars like Baby Ruth and Mr. Goodbar.

Mr. Laurier, always suave and dapper in his white shirt and black bow tie, paid me two dollars and fifty cents a week, and treated me to a chocolate frappe on Saturday afternoon after handing me the money.

Nicole Renard dropped into the drugstore once in a while. She sometimes lingered after picking out her favorite candy. Butterscotch Bits, three for a penny. She, too, had discovered the Monument Public Library and told me how she wept as she read the final pages of *A Farewell to Arms*.

"That's my favorite novel," I said.

"Have you read *Rebecca*?" she asked.

"No, but I saw the movie," I replied, amazed that we were carrying on a normal conversation.

"I did, too, but I liked the book better," she said. "Which do you like best, movies or books?"

"Both," I said.

"Me too."

And then a sudden silence but a good silence as she offered me a Butterscotch Bit.

Taking a deep breath, I said: "Would you like to go to the movies sometime?"

The earth paused in its orbit.

"That would be nice," she said at last.

Saturday afternoons at the Plymouth downtown became our weekly date—the word made my head spin: I was actually dating Nicole Renard. We met in front of the theater and she insisted on buying her own ticket although she allowed me to treat her to Milk Duds from the vending machine in the lobby. The theater was always crowded and raucous, the Saturday matinees a special time for kids, with a cowboy serial and two movies. The Movietone News brought reminders of the war that was raging around the globe, as the grim narrator spoke of places that had been unknown to us a few months ago—Bataan in the Pacific, Tobruk in Africa. We cheered our fighting forces and booed and hissed when Hitler came on the screen, his arm always raised in that hated salute.

At some point during the afternoon we held hands, her hand cool in my own, but I had to keep drawing mine away to wipe the sweat from my palm. Just before "The End" of the last movie appeared on the screen, she allowed me an innocent kiss, our lips briefly touching, the taste of chocolate transferred from her lips to mine. Once, my hand accidentally dropped and brushed her sweater and I was surprised at the softness of her breast.

My hand lingered there for a moment and she didn't protest. My breath went away and then came back again as we rose to leave.

On the way home, we talked not only about the movies we had seen but about a thousand other things. I was amazed at the lack of pauses in our conversation, how I always managed to have something to say. She had a way of teasing that coaxed me into forgetting my shyness.

"What do you want to do besides be a champion at table tennis?"

"I don't know." My mind racing: What *did* I want to do?

"You must want to do something, Francis. Say the first thing that comes into your mind."

"I want to read every book in the Monument Public Library."

"Good," she said. "How about writing books? Didn't you win Sister Mathilde's medal for composition?"

A blush of both pleasure and embarrassment made my cheeks grow warm.

"Oh, I could never write a book."

"I think you could."

It was necessary to change the subject: "How about you, Nicole? What do you want to do?"

"Oh, lots of things," she said, raising her head and looking round at the passing Frenchtown three-deckers, the steeple of St. Jude's in the distance. "Such a big world out there. I'd like to help more in the war. Maybe become a nurse, if the war lasts long enough . . ."

I knew that she spent time with the nuns at the convent, knitting socks and scarves for the armed forces. I teased her about the smell of cooked cabbage that she carried with her when she dropped in to Laurier's after leaving the convent. "The convent's perfume," I said, thinking myself clever.

"Not a bad smell, Francis," she said. "Better than Evening in Paris." Which was the cheap perfume that was our best-seller at the store.

Once, as we passed the Wreck Center, I started to sing "Dancing in the Dark" in a comic way, off-key as usual, because I loved to hear her laugh. But she didn't laugh this time.

"That was a sad party, wasn't it?" she said.

I agreed, thinking of that December seventh party, during which word was received that the Japanese had bombed a place we'd never heard of called Pearl Harbor, the party suddenly frivolous and superfluous. How could we celebrate a table tennis tournament and a musical show when our country had been attacked and our world had changed so drastically in the space of a few moments?

The party broke up abruptly as everyone left to go home, hurrying through the streets as if bombers were expected to fly over Frenchtown at any minute. We had discovered in one moment on a Sunday afternoon that the world was not a safe place anymore.

Laurier's Drug Store became the gathering spot for the people of Frenchtown, who bought *The Mon-*

ument Times or *The Wickburg Telegram* and discussed the progress of the war, shaking their heads at the swiftness with which the boys of Frenchtown were becoming fighting men.

"Amazing," Mr. Laurier said. "A kid graduates from high school, gets six weeks of basic training with guns and grenades, then overseas he goes on a troopship and five months later—five months later!—he's fighting the Japs or the Germans."

The small red radio on the shelf near the soda fountain blared the news of the day between wartime songs like "Rosie the Riveter," which celebrated the working women in the war factories, and "The White Cliffs of Dover," about the cliffs the fliers saw as they returned to England after bombing raids over Europe.

Every day, page five of the *Times* carried stories and pictures of our fighting forces, often announcing medals awarded for valor on the battlefields.

"Did you hear about Larry LaSalle?" Nicole asked breathlessly, rushing into the store one Tuesday afternoon. Although she was speaking to me at the candy counter, the customers turned and listened and a deep silence fell in the store.

"He saved the lives of an entire platoon," she announced. "Captured an enemy machine-gun nest. It was on the radio . . ."

The following Saturday afternoon at the Plymouth, we were stunned to suddenly see Larry LaSalle featured in the Movietone News. He was unshaven, face gaunt and drawn, eyes sunk deep into their sockets. But it was our Larry LaSalle, all right.

Cheers filled the air, feet stomped the floor, almost drowning out the voice of the broadcaster:

"A New England marine is one of the great heroes of Pacific action, receiving the Silver Star . . ." and again cheers and applause rocked the theater, drowning out the rest of the commentary.

That night and the following day, the people of Monument jammed the Plymouth to see the town's first big war hero on the silver screen.

I haven't always worn the scarf and the bandage. In the hospital in England, on its grounds and in the surrounding countryside, I enjoyed the sting of air on my flesh, once the bandages were removed. I had barely glimpsed myself in mirrors, windows or glass doors. Until the day I went on a three-day pass in London.

Walking through the bright sunshine of a spring

day, I was disappointed because London had always been linked in my mind with foggy days and evenings and either Jack the Ripper or Sherlock Holmes stalking through the shadows. I headed for Baker Street, hoping to find 221B, even though I knew that address existed only in the stories of Conan Doyle.

As I walked along, I became aware of people coming upon me and turning away, or giving me wide walking space. A small boy holding his mother's hand suddenly cried out and pushed his face into his mother's skirt. I wondered what had scared him until I saw him peeking at me again with one big eye before bursting into tears.

I shrank against the side of a building and made my way to the plate-glass window of a pub, where, among the advertisements for pints of ale and kidney pies, I saw what the boy had seen—my face. No face at all, actually, the nostrils like the snout of an animal, the peeling cheeks, the toothless gums, my jaw and mouth jammed together as if by invisible clamps.

I tried to draw up the collar of my Eisenhower jacket to cover at least the lower part of my face but the collar was too narrow, didn't cover anything at all, and I hurried along the sidewalk, head down, avoiding eye contact, wishing to be invisible.

Why didn't anyone warn me? I wondered bitterly on the double-decker bus, hiding my face in my hands. Then realized that the doctors and nurses had probably become so accustomed to the wounded and the maimed that the abnormal had become normal to them.

Enrico made me the gift of the white scarf, which he said he had won from an air force flyboy in a poker game.

Now in Frenchtown, my face is healing. My dentures have given shape to the lower part of my face and my jaw is firmer, but my nostrils are still caves and the flesh of my cheeks refuses to heal completely, remaining raw and red. When I study myself in the mirror, I don't see *me* anymore but a stranger slowly taking shape.

The truth is that I don't care whether I heal or not. Because I know that it doesn't matter. What matters is hiding my face from others, not only to save them the shock of seeing a face in disrepair but so that they won't identify little Francis Cassavant later on, after I have carried out my mission.

Now each day when I wake up I know that this might be the day when Larry LaSalle will show up and I start to close doors. Not real doors but doors to the future. I take out the address and telephone number of Dr. Abrams in Kansas City and burn it in the kitchen sink. Next is the list of veterans' hospitals that Enrico handed to me when I left England. "I'll be in one of them," he told me, "until I find the proper method of disposal." I knew what he meant by disposal because I had already planned my own method after my mission was completed.

I watch the flames eating up the list of hospitals. *Goodbye, Enrico.*

The smell of ashes fills the air, a damp incense burning for Larry LaSalle's homecoming.

His second homecoming.

Closing my eyes, I think of Nicole and how his first homecoming during the war changed our lives forever.

Lieutenant Lawrence LaSalle, U.S. Marine Corps, holder of the Silver Star for acts of heroism in the steaming jungles of Guadalcanal in the South Pacific, hero of newsreels and radio broadcasts, was coming home on furlough. He was scheduled to arrive on the 3:10 P.M. train from Boston on July 3, 1943.

On that hot and humid afternoon, a crowd gathered at the Monument Depot to greet his arrival, including kids from the Wreck Center, Joey Le-Blanc, Louis Arabelle, Marie LaCroix and me among them, and parents who knew that Larry LaSalle had been a bright Pied Piper for their children in the bleakness of the Depression.

I looked toward Monument Park, impatient for Nicole to join us. As a volunteer now with the Monument Red Cross, she was preparing food kits for servicemen that day and said she would join us in time for Larry LaSalle's arrival.

I placed a foot on the rail, hoping to feel the slight trembling that would announce the train's approach. The heat of the rail burned through the sole of my shoe. Turning, I saw Nicole coming into view through the haze of heat. She wore a dark blue skirt and a white blouse. She waved to me as she hurried toward the depot. At the same time, the chug of engine, blast of horn and hiss of steam announced the arrival of the train from Boston.

A moment later Larry LaSalle stood on the platform, resplendent in the green uniform with the lieutenant's bars on his shoulders and the ribbons and medals on his chest. He smiled, the old movie-star smile, skin tanned and glowing, small wrinkles around his eyes as he squinted down at us.

We cheered as he stepped down from the platform and walked toward our group, that touch of Fred Astaire still in his walk but something different about him. His slenderness was knifelike now, lethal, his features sharper, nose and cheekbones. I remembered how hard it had been to think of him as a fighting marine when he announced his enlistment but seeing his lean hard body now I could picture him storming a hillside on Guadalcanal, rifle in hand, bayonet fixed, grenades dangling from his belt, pumping bullets into the enemy.

Then he was among us and we surrounded him, crowding him, embracing him, getting as close to him as possible.

"My hero from the war," Joey LeBlanc called out, clowning, of course, but saying what we all thought. Larry was our war hero, yes, but he had been a hero to us long before he went to war.

He drew away, holding us off at arm's length, stepping back. "The better to see you," he said, looking at each of us in turn. When his eyes fell on me, I made a gesture, as if serving the small white ball over the net, and he swiveled his arm, as if returning the ball. His eyes moved to Nicole and I saw the rush of affection on his face. Nicole bowed, tilting her head like a ballet dancer, and he dipped his head in return, his eyes full of her. A blush turned her cheeks crimson and only added to her beauty.

Mayor Harold Burnham arrived in a big black car, followed by city officials, most of whom walked the short distance from City Hall. Car horns blew and more cheers rose in the afternoon heat as the mayor vigorously shook Larry LaSalle's hand, embraced him fiercely and presented him with a silver key to the city.

"You are our celebration," the mayor declared, referring to the fact that holidays were observed quietly during the war years. No bonfires or fireworks and no parades. "Your presence in this great city of ours, Lieutenant Lawrence LaSalle, is cause enough for jubilation." Other officials made speeches, and the words sailed over our heads meaninglessly, while Larry LaSalle stood modestly before the crowd, eyes lowered. Finally, a stillness fell and he turned to the gathering. "Thank you," he said.

He spoke of the men and women serving in all parts of the globe who were defending freedom and how some of them would give their lives, willingly and courageously. He paused and looked down at us, his kids from the Wreck Center.

"I'm glad to be home, even if it's only for a little while. And most of all I want to be with the Wreck Center gang."

Once again, he had made us feel special, singling us out from the townspeople who gathered there. Nicole squeezed my hand and my eyes grew moist.

"We have to keep the world safe for these young people—they are our future . . ."

The celebration went on during the afternoon and evening, culminating in a Welcome Home dance that night at City Hall. The hall was a bright spot in the dark wartime city, streetlights dim, air-raid wardens patrolling the peak of Moosock Hill on the lookout for enemy planes, although an air attack on Monument was a remote possibility. But better be vigilant than sorry, said an editorial in *The Monument Times*. German U-boats had been sighted in the waters off the Massachusetts shore and rumors claimed that Nazis prowled the streets of New England in disguise. But City Hall blazed with lights behind the blackout curtains and the big orchestra played the tunes of the day while the dancers twirled on the floor.

We were a merry group, Larry LaSalle's guests at the dance. Sitting in a special section of the balcony, we looked down as he moved among the city officials and their wives, shaking hands, enduring slaps on the back, the embraces of beautiful women. I glanced occasionally at Nicole as she gazed, wide-eyed and wistful, at the ladies in their fancy gowns, glittery sequins catching the lights from a crystal ball revolving on the ceiling.

"Isn't that beautiful?" Nicole said, pointing to a woman in a simple white gown that clung to her body like whipped cream.

"I'll buy you one like that someday," I whispered in her ear, my voice trembling a bit, betraying my love for her.

Squeezing my hand, she leaned toward me, and her warm cheek rested against mine.

Finally, Larry LaSalle looked up and motioned toward the front of the hall, meaning he wanted us to join him there. He met us at the entrance, the music muted in the background, and announced:

"A surprise awaits."

With a flourish, he led us outside and down the City Hall steps.

He lined us up and we began a wild snake dance through Monument Square, among the statues of generals and the Civil War cannon and by the water fountain. Larry LaSalle headed the line; Nicole was next with her hands on his hips and mine on hers. We laughed and yelled and stopped at the fountain to drink and splash our faces, then crossed the intersection of Main and West and began to march down Mechanic Street, breaking ranks occasionally to pause and laugh, as if we were all drunk without having taken a sip of liquor.

Once, Nicole whispered: "Stay close to me," as we resumed our parade in the shadowed streets, and a thrill went through me like a jolt as I pulled her close and said: "I'll never leave you." As if we were living a love scene at the Plymouth.

Finally, the big surprise was at hand as Larry led us along Third Street until we stood in front of the Wreck Center. He bowed to us, produced a key from his pocket, unlocked the door and swung it open.

"Voilà," he said, ushering us inside. And then told us he had arranged for Henry Roussier, the old retired janitor, to sweep and clean up the center for a special night. When Larry turned on the lights, we saw the Ping-Pong table, rackets and white balls on it. A table with cans of soda pop and candy bars, not chocolate bars anymore because of wartime restrictions, but candy all the same. Larry placed a record on the phonograph and the hall was filled with an old song from the bright and exciting days of the Wreck Center, before the war, in the time of table tennis tournaments and *Follies and Fancies* musicals.

Never in a million years
Will there be another you . . .

We played table tennis without keeping score, hitting the ball back and forth, trying for and sometimes making impossible shots, Larry rolling up the sleeves of his shirt, removing the medals and ribbons that he called scrambled eggs. We played game after game while Nicole changed the records and jitterbugged with Marie LaCroix.

The evening wore down and Joey LeBlanc and Louis Arabelle said good night and later Marie and the others wandered off until finally there were only Larry and Nicole and me. He embraced us both. "My favorite champion and my favorite dancer," he said.

"Find 'Dancing in the Dark,'" he told Nicole.

As she went off to search among the records, Larry placed his arm around my shoulder. "Time to go home, Francis," he said. "You look tired . . . it's been a long day."

The day had not been long enough for me.

"I don't mind staying," I said.

"Nicole and I are going to have one last dance," he said. "Just her and me alone. It's important, Francis."

I wondered if he had a big announcement for her. That he had found a way to make her a star. Entertaining the troops, maybe. Nothing was impossible with Larry LaSalle. His face was flushed and his eyes shone with excitement. "So, you'd better go, okay?"

Nicole placed the record on the spindle and turned toward us, an expectant look on her face, glancing at Larry.

"I've got to go," I told her. "You and Larry stay. One last dance . . ." The words sounded false as I said them and I realized they were Larry's words, not mine.

Nicole frowned. "Stay and watch," she said, and I was puzzled by the expression on her face. Was she only being polite, asking me to stay? Did she want to be alone with Larry?

He went to her, placed his arm around her, drawing her to him gently. "He's tired," Larry said. "He wants to go . . ."

We always did what Larry LaSalle told us to do. Always carried out his slightest wish. And now I seemed actually to be tired, as Larry had suggested, the events of the day and all the excitement catching up to me. I saw Larry raising his eyebrows at me, the way he looked at me when I made a stupid move at table tennis. *Get going . . .*

"I'd better go," I said, keeping my eyes away from Nicole, a pang of regret gnawing at me even as I spoke, because I really wanted to stay, wanted to be a part of them.

As I turned away I heard the plop the record made, dropping onto the turntable. A patter of feet, then a hand touched my shoulder.

"Don't go," Nicole whispered into my ear.

But Larry LaSalle had told me to go.

"No, I'd better leave," I said. "I think he wants to tell you something."

The first notes of "Dancing in the Dark" filled the air, and the singer sang:

> Dancing in the dark
> Till the tune ends . . .

Suddenly, he was there, sweeping her into his arms, and as he did so, he reached out and flicked the switch, plunging the hall into darkness. I made my way toward the front door but drew back, didn't leave, stationed myself in the small foyer, in a slant of moonlight, as the music filled the place, miserable in my aloneness, wanting to be dancing with her, the way Larry LaSalle was dancing with her, holding her close.

In the shadows of the hallway, I stood in agony and waited for the song to end, and then I would tell Nicole that I had not left, that I had stayed, would never desert her, that she had told me not to go and I hadn't, that she was more important to me than Larry LaSalle.

The song ended and the scratching of the needle on the record did not stop and I heard a sigh and a sound that could have been a moan and a rustle of clothing.

How long did I stand there listening? Hearing the small sounds, then a sudden gasp, and the needle scratching as the record went round and round, and I couldn't breathe, my body rigid, my lungs burning, and at the moment of panic, heart thudding, my breath returned, and I listened and heard nothing now. What were they doing? But I knew what they were doing—the thought streaked through my mind so fast that it could hardly be acknowledged.

Then, a whimpering, like a small animal caught and trapped, moaning distinct now. The scratching of the needle stopped. Footsteps approaching, coming close, closer, and suddenly she stumbled into the hallway, her face caught in the slash of moonlight.

She saw me the moment I saw her. Saw her face, her eyes. Her hair disheveled, mouth flung open, lips swollen. Cheeks moist with tears. Her white blouse torn and one hand clutching the front of her blouse to hold it together.

I drew out of the darkness toward her and she raised a hand to stop me, gasping now, her breath like a moan escaping her body.

In the spill of moonlight, her eyes flashed black with anger as she looked at me. More than anger. But what? What? I brought my hand up to my face, not to brush away my own tears but to hide from her terrible gaze. But I couldn't cover my eyes, had to look at her. And I recognized in her eyes now what I could not deny: betrayal. My betrayal of her in her eyes.

For another long moment she stared at me, mouth still agape, then shook her head as if in disbelief and fled toward the door, fumbling with the doorknob. She pulled the door open, stepped through, slamming the door behind her while I stood there helplessly.

Numb, I stepped out of the moonlight's rays, wanting to hide in the dark.

Larry's voice called from inside the hall.

"Anybody there?"

I stood hushed, pressed to the wall, heard my own breathing so harsh that I was afraid he could hear it. His footsteps grew louder as he approached. He passed through the flash of moonlight, a ghostly silhouette, and I closed my eyes, not wanting to see him. Then, no footsteps. Had he seen me? My eyes flew open. He was at the door, a shadow now, turning the knob, whistling a tune . . . "Dancing in the Dark" . . . whistling softly as he stepped through the doorway, closing the door gently behind him, and went off into the night.

I stood there thinking of what I had seen in Nicole's eyes.

It's amazing that the heart makes no noise when it cracks.

A heat wave gripped Frenchtown, the heat almost visible in the air. People moved as if in a slow-motion movie, gathering on front lawns and piazzas in the evening after the shops closed, hoping for a breeze to cool them off. Men walked slowly as they went off to work in the shops as weary looking in the morning as they were late in the day after their shifts were over.

For three days, I haunted Sixth Street at all hours, standing across the street and looking up at the second floor of Nicole's house, venturing sometimes into the yard, hoping that I might catch a glimpse of her coming or going or at a window. Despite the heat, the piazza on Nicole's second-floor tenement remained vacant. The windows were open to allow cooler air to enter the tenement but no one came or went.

Nicole's father left the tenement to go to the shop just before seven o'clock in the morning and returned shortly after five in the afternoon and I avoided him, kept away from the street during those times.

A small boy in the house across the street from Nicole's rode his bicycle endlessly on the sidewalk and gazed at me occasionally as I waited. Finally, squinting against the sun, he asked: "Why are you here all the time?"

I shrugged. "Waiting."

"Are you the boogeyman?" he asked, scratching his chin.

Yes, I wanted to say. A kind of boogeyman who does terrible things like letting his girl get hurt and attacked, purposely avoiding even in my mind that terrible word: what had actually happened to her.

The boy waited a moment for my reply, then pedaled back into his yard, silent as he gazed at me over his shoulder. He went into the house and did not come out again.

• • •

In Laurier's Drug Store, rumors were rampant about Larry LaSalle's sudden departure from Frenchtown so soon after his arrival. Someone said his furlough had been canceled, that his outfit had been recalled to duty for a big push in Europe against the Nazis. There was talk of a Western Union messenger bicycling down Mechanic Street in the middle of the night, bringing a telegram to the tenement Larry LaSalle rented on Spruce Street.

"That wasn't a messenger," Mr. Laurier scoffed. "That was Crazy Joe Touraine trying to cool off from the heat of the day . . ."

I could not sleep at night. Lay on the bed and stared up at the ceiling, glad for the heat that was so relentless, as if it were part of the hell that I had earned.

• • •

Finally, on the fourth day, I saw her emerging from the hallway to the piazza on the first floor.

She did not move away as I came into the yard.

"Nicole," I called.

She saw me, frowned, drew back a step, then paused, as if waiting for me to approach.

"Nicole." My voice breaking, not like the days

of my shyness with her but because my heart was so full it destroyed her name as I spoke it.

Her eyes met mine. She didn't say anything for a long moment and when she finally spoke, her voice was harsh.

"You were there all the time," she said.

I couldn't reply, could find no words to utter in my defense. Because I had no defense.

"You didn't do anything."

The accusation in her voice was worse than the harshness.

"I know." I wasn't sure whether I spoke those words or only thought them.

"You knew what he was doing, didn't you?"

My head so heavy, pounding with blood, that I could barely nod in agreement.

Leaning against the banister, she asked: "Why didn't you do something? Tell him to stop. Run for help. Anything."

"I'm sorry," I said, knowing how pitiful those words must sound to her.

She shook her head, turning away, and I couldn't afford to let her go.

"Are you . . . ," I began to ask, but hesitated as she turned back and looked at me again. What word could I use? Are you hurt? Torn apart?

"Are you all right?" I asked.

"No, I'm not all right," she answered, anger flashing in her eyes. "I hurt. I hurt all over."

I could only stand there mute, as if all my sins had been revealed and there was no forgiveness for them.

Finally, I asked: "What can I do?"

"Poor Francis," she said at last. But no pity in her voice. Contempt, maybe, as her eyes swept me. She flung her hand in the air, a gesture of dismissal. "Go away, Francis," she said. "Just go away."

And she herself went away, pulled away from the banister, stepped into the hallway, one moment there, the next moment gone.

I waited for her to appear again.

I waited through long empty minutes.

Somewhere a door slammed. Later, a dog barked, a car roared by.

I finally went away.

• • •

Later that week, I went to church after supper and slipped into Father Balthazar's confessional, waiting there until Mr. Boudreau, the janitor, closed the doors for the night. Finally I stepped out into the old smell of burning wax and incense and walked through the shadows to the back of the church. I climbed the stairs to the choir loft and opened the door that led to the exterior of the tallest steeple. Father Balthazar had shown me the door during my altar boy days.

I started climbing in the darkness, up the steep steps that workers climbed to repair portions of the steeple. The heat intensified and the stairs narrowed as I ascended, my heart beating heavily, my breath coming in gasps, the sound like cloth ripping.

Pausing to gather strength and wait for my heart and lungs to calm down a bit, I looked for the stone door that could be swiveled aside to allow access to the outer surface of the steeple. My fingers found it. Grunting, gasping, I managed to move it aside on its rusty hinges. I looked out at Frenchtown below me, the dark shapes of the three-deckers, the shadowed streets, the stars closer than I'd ever seen them as if I could reach out and pluck one of them from the sky.

Despite the calmness of the summer night, a gust of wind caught me by surprise, cooling the perspiration on my face and forehead. I rested there, bathing in the sudden coolness. Then peered out again, craning my neck to look down at the cement sidewalk below. How long would it take to plunge toward the sidewalk? Still staring down, I began to mumble a prayer, in French, the old *Notre Père*, the way the nuns had taught us, then stopped, horrified at what I was doing. Saying a prayer before committing the worst sin of all: despair. I thought of St. Jude's Cemetery and the pitiful graves set apart from the rest, the ones who had taken their own lives and could not be buried in consecrated ground. I thought of my mother and father—could I disgrace their name this way? *Did you hear what Lefty's son did last night, jumped to his death from the steeple of St. Jude's?*

I could not die that way. Soldiers were dying with honor on battlefields all over the world. Noble deaths. The deaths of heroes. How could I die by leaping from a steeple?

The next afternoon I boarded the bus to Fort Delta, in my pocket the birth certificate I had altered to change my age, and became a soldier in the United States Army.

I always thought I would spot Larry LaSalle on Third Street, would see him striding along like Fred Astaire, bestowing that movie-star smile on people he met. I would shadow him through the streets and follow him home, note his address, and then return late with the gun in my pocket, ready to do my job.

Instead, I learn of his return from, of all people,

Mrs. Belander, as I come back from another round of searching the Frenchtown streets.

I overhear her talking to a neighbor as they stand on the back porch. Mrs. Belander is folding clothes she has drawn off the clothesline that links her house with the three-decker next door. The neighbor is Mrs. Agneaux, a big woman with flushed cheeks and bulging eyes. They are talking in French and I linger nearby, listening like a spy. They don't realize that I understand most of what they are saying as they talk of the weather and then of old Mr. Tardier, who likes to pinch women on the *derrière* when they pass.

I am stunned when I hear the name of Larry LaSalle on the lips of Mrs. Agneaux.

The French language spoken by Canadians passes quickly on their tongues, almost like music, sometimes so quickly that the words are lost as they cascade in the air. I draw closer to catch every syllable and miss some of them but hear enough to make my heart begin to race and my flesh to grow warm. I am concentrating so hard that a headache begins, a throbbing pain above my eyes.

What I obtain from Mrs. Agneaux's quick tongue is that Larry LaSalle has returned to Frenchtown, he walks slowly as if his legs hurt, he is living in the second-floor tenement of a three-decker owned by someone whose name I don't catch, on the corner of Ninth and Spruce.

"Which corner?" Mrs. Belander, bless her, asks the question I myself want to ask.

"The green house, cheap paint, bought discount, fading already . . ."

But I don't hear the rest of her description.

I have heard enough.

Larry LaSalle has returned to Frenchtown.

And I know where to find him.

The gun is like a tumor on my thigh as I walk through the morning streets against the wind that never dies down. April sunlight stings my eyes but the wind dissipates its heat, blustering against store windows and kicking debris into the gutters.

At Ninth and Spruce, I pause and look up at the three-decker and the windows of the second floor, where Larry LaSalle can be found at last. Does he suspect my presence here on the street? Does he have a premonition that he has only a few minutes left to live?

I am calm. My heartbeat is normal. What's one more death after the others in the villages and fields of France? The innocent faces of the two young Germans appear in my mind. But Larry LaSalle is not innocent.

The steps leading to the second floor are worn from use and age, and I think of all the people who have climbed stairs like these, who have worked in the shops and come home heavy with weariness at the end of the day. As I stand at the door of Larry LaSalle's tenement, I touch the bulge in my pocket to verify the existence of the gun. The sound of my knocking is loud and commanding in the silent hallway.

No response. I wait. I rap on the door again, hand clenched as a fist this time.

"Come on in, the door's not locked," Larry LaSalle calls out. That voice is unmistakable, a bit feeble now, yet still the voice that cheered us at the Wreck Center.

Hesitant suddenly, uncertain—his voice giving reality to what I must do—I step into the tenement and into the fragrance of pea soup simmering on the black stove, steam rising from a big green pot.

He is sitting in a rocking chair by the black coal

stove, and narrows his eyes, squinting to see who has come into his tenement. He is pale, eyes sunk into his sockets like in the newsreel at the Plymouth, and he seems fragile now, as if caught in an old photograph that has faded and yellowed with age. His eyes blink rapidly as if taking quick pictures of me. Is there a glimmer of fear in his eyes? My heart quickens at the possibility.

"Francis, Francis Cassavant," I announce. It's important for him to know immediately who I am. I don't want to waste any time.

"Ah, Francis," he says, his eyes flashing pleasure because he doesn't sense my mission.

"Come in, come in," he says, the old enthusiasm back in his voice.

He rises slowly from the chair, steadying the rocker as he lifts himself up. As he holds out his hands in greeting, I go forward to meet him. We shake hands. At the last minute, when it seems we might embrace as old friends and comrades, teacher and pupil, I pull away. His white hands clutch the air before he clasps them together and settles back into the chair.

"Sit, sit," he says, indicating the chair next to the window opposite his own.

"Take off your jacket," he says. "Your Red Sox cap, too, and your scarf . . ."

I don't move. I don't take off anything. I don't

plan to stay long, only long enough to carry out my mission.

"Don't be afraid to show your face, Francis. That face, what's left of it, is a symbol of how brave you were, the Silver Star you earned . . ."

"You earned a Silver Star, too," I say, having to reply, and marveling again how Larry LaSalle was always one step ahead of us just as he now knows about my face and the Silver Star.

He shrugs, sagging in the chair, sighing, as if tired suddenly.

"It's good of you to visit . . . ," he says, smiling the old movie-star smile. "Makes me remember the old days at the Wreck Center. Those were good days, weren't they? That table tennis championship. What a great day for you, Francis . . ."

A deep sadness settles on me, as if winter has invaded my bones.

"You made it possible. You let me win."

"You miss the point, Francis. You deserved to win. It was more than a game. More than a score. You played like a champion and deserved the trophy . . ."

Why did it have to turn out like this!

"But those days are gone now. And the war is over. Everything's different. Not only the war but everything," he says. Lifting his hands, he studies them. Then looks down at his body. He rubs his thighs. "No wounds that you can see, Francis. But I'm worn out. They called it jungle fever at first but I don't think they really know what it is . . ."

Maybe your sins catching up with you.

"And you, Francis. Will you be okay? Will you heal? Be like new again?"

"Yes." I don't feel like going into all the details or telling him about Dr. Abrams because it's not going to happen, anyway.

Silence falls in the room and he shifts his body in the chair. I touch the gun in my pocket to remind me of my mission.

"How did you get in the army so young?" he asks, focusing his eyes on me, the way he did in the old days, as if my words were the most important he had ever heard.

I tell him about the forged papers. "They were taking anybody with a heartbeat in those days."

"Just a kid." Shaking his head, his eyes alight with admiration. "And you became a hero . . ."

I had always wanted to be a hero, like Larry LaSalle and all the others, but have been a fake all along. And now I am tired of the deception and have to rid myself of the fakery.

I look away from him, out the window at the sun-splashed street. "I'm not a hero," I tell him.

"Of course you are. I heard about you, read the stories in the newspapers . . ."

"Know why I went to war?"

"Why does anybody go to war, Francis?"

"I went to war because I wanted to die." Lowering my voice as if in the confessional with Father Balthazar: "I was too much of a coward to kill myself. In the war, in a battle, I figured it would be easy to get killed. And I wouldn't be disgracing my father and mother's name. I looked for chances to die and instead killed others, and two of them kids like me . . ."

"You saved your patrol. You fell on that grenade . . ."

"When I fell on that grenade, I wasn't trying to save those GIs. I saw my chance to end it all, in a second. But a freak accident happened. My face got blown off and I didn't die . . ."

His voice is a whisper: "Why did you want to die, Francis?"

"Don't you know?" Stunned by his question, then realizing that he hadn't seen me that night.

"Nicole. Nicole Renard."

His mouth drops open and he flinches as if reeling from an unexpected blow.

"I stayed behind that night." My own voice is now a whisper. "I heard what you were doing to her.

And I saw her afterward. Those eyes of hers and what was in them . . ."

Shaking his head, he says: "You wanted to die because of that?"

I still want to die.

"What you did to her. And I did nothing. Just stood there and let it happen . . ."

"Oh, Francis. You're too hard on yourself. You didn't do anything you should feel guilty about, that should make you want to die. You couldn't have stopped me, anyway, Francis. You were just a child . . ."

"So was she." My lips trembling.

A long sigh escapes him.

"Is that why you came here? To tell me this?"

I take the gun out of my pocket.

"Here's why I came."

I aim the gun at him, my finger on the trigger.

But my hand is shaking and my caves are running and I am suddenly overwhelmed by the knowledge of what I am about to do. Why has it come to this?

"You could have had anybody," I say, my voice too loud, booming in my ears. "All those beautiful ladies at the dance that night. Why Nicole?"

"The sweet young things, Francis. Even their heat is sweet . . ."

Sweet young things. Had he done it before? How many young girls had been invaded by him?

I shake my head in dismay.

"Everybody sins, Francis. The terrible thing is that we love our sins. We love the thing that makes us evil. I love the sweet young things."

"That isn't love," I say.

"There's all kinds of love, Francis."

"Then, didn't you know that we loved you?" I say. "You were our hero, even before you went to war. You made us better than we were . . ."

He sighs, his lips trembling, and his voice trembles, too, when he asks:

"Does that one sin of mine wipe away all the good things?"

"That's a question you should ask Nicole," I say, my eyes measuring him. Until this moment I haven't planned where I will place the bullet, whether to aim for that spot between the eyes or for his chest, his heart. It isn't a question of aiming, really, not at this distance. Only desire. The desire to avenge what he did to Nicole and to the other young girls, now that I know about them.

He waves his hand at me, as if dismissing the gun in my hand.

"Know why I'm sitting in this chair, Francis? And barely stood up when you came in? My legs are gone." He gestures toward the table and I notice for the first time the aluminum crutch leaning against the table. "No more dancing for me, Francis. No more sweet young things. No more anything."

"Am I supposed to feel bad for you?"

"Don't look at me like that," he says, turning his eyes away from me. "If I wanted one thing, it would be to have you look at me again the way you did at the Wreck Center. When I was the big hero you say I was. But it's too late, isn't it?"

I am tired of this talk, impatient to do what I've come here to do.

"Say your prayers," I tell him, just as I've rehearsed those words so many times through the years. I've decided to aim for the heart after all, to shatter his heart the way he broke Nicole's and mine—and how many others?

"Wait," he calls out, reaching toward a small table next to his chair and a cigar box on the table. He opens the box and withdraws a pistol, like my own, a relic of the war.

I flinch, my finger agitated on the trigger, but he places the gun in his lap, cradling it in his hand.

"You see, Francis. I have my own gun. I take it out and look at it all the time. I place it against my temple once in a while. I wonder how it would feel to pull the trigger and have everything come to an end." He sighs and shakes his head, then nods toward me. "So lower your gun, Francis, one gun is enough for what has to be done."

He sees the doubt in my eyes and, in a swift movement, removes the magazine from his pistol.

"Empty," he says. "You're safe, Francis. You were always safe with me. So put your gun away. Whether you know it or not, you've accomplished your mission here. And you couldn't have killed me anyway, in cold blood."

We stare at each other for a long moment.

"Please," he says, and his voice is like the cry of a small child.

I lower the gun. I remove my finger from the trigger. My hand trembles. I put the gun back in my pocket.

"Go, Francis. Leave me here. Leave everything here, the war, what happened at the Wreck Center, leave it all behind, with me."

Suddenly, I only want to get out of there. The aroma of the soup is sickening and the tenement is too warm. I don't want to look into his eyes anymore.

My hand is on the doorknob when he calls my name. I open the door but pause, making myself wait. But I don't look at him.

"Let me tell you one thing before you go, Francis. You would have fallen on that grenade anyway.

All your instincts would have made you sacrifice yourself for your comrades."

Still trying to make me better than I am.

I close the door, my face hot and flushed under the scarf and the bandage. The coldness of the hallway hits the warmth of my flesh and I shiver. It seems as if I have done nothing but shiver since I returned to Frenchtown.

His voice echoes in my ears:

Does that one sin of mine wipe away all the good things?

I go down the stairs, my footsteps echoing on the worn staircase.

Downstairs, at last, after what seems like a long, long time, I pause at the outside door. The sound of a pistol shot cracks the air. My hand is on the doorknob. The sound from this distance is almost like that of a Ping-Pong ball striking the table.

The sound of the doorbell echoes unendingly through the long corridors of the convent. Waiting, I step back and look at the faded redbrick exterior of the building and the black forbidding shutters at the windows. On summer evenings, we played our games—Buck, Buck, How Many Fingers Up? and Kick the Can—in the schoolyard until a nun threw open the shutters, clapped her hands and sent us scurrying home in the gathering twilight.

The door opens and an old nun with transparent skin looks suspiciously at me. I am accustomed by now to the shock my appearance gives people and try to make my voice gentle and unthreatening.

"Is it possible to speak to Sister Mathilde? I'm one of her former pupils."

She studies me for a long moment with her pale blue eyes, then gestures to me to step inside. She ushers me to a small room to the right of the foyer. The familiar smell of strong soap and cabbage cooking hangs heavy in the air.

Nodding toward one of the two straight-backed chairs near the window, she waits until I sit down before turning away. She hasn't spoken a word. Her footsteps fade as I settle myself in the chair, wondering if I am on a futile errand. I am here because I remember how often Nicole visited the nuns in the convent, strolled the grounds with Sister Mathilde and knitted socks and scarves for servicemen with the sisters. I wonder if Sister Mathilde might know what happened to Nicole or where her family moved.

The whisper of starched clothing and the clump of heavy shoes announce Sister Mathilde's arrival. As she enters the room, she touches the long black rosary beads that dangle from her hip to the hem of her long black skirt. Her skin is as white as the starched wimple framing her face.

She regards me curiously and I take off the Red Sox cap. "Francis Cassavant," I say.

"Of course, Francis," she says, a smile lighting up her eyes. She seldom smiled in the classroom. "I hear you served your country well. You have made us all proud."

She sits on the edge of the chair as if being a nun does not allow her to sit comfortably. "We still pray for our men and women in uniform every day and night."

She asks about my wounds and I tell her as little as possible. She says she will offer up special prayers for me. Finally, a question appears in her eyes.

"Nicole Renard," I say. "I have been wondering where she is and what she's doing. Her family left town while I was away. Do you know where they went, Sister?"

"Nicole, yes," she says, nodding her head. "You were friends, *n'est-ce pas?*"

I nod in return, my interest quickening.

"Ah, Nicole," she says, clasping her hands and then unclasping them. "A good girl. Smart. A secretive girl, too. But then, we all have secrets, eh, Francis?"

I shrug, not daring to say anything. A thought strikes me.

"Has she gone away to become a nun?" I ask. The possibility dashes my hopes of ever seeing her again.

"She's gone away, yes, but not to become a nun," Sister Mathilde says. "Life is not that simple, Francis, and neither is a calling to God."

Glad that my face is behind the scarf and the bandage so that she can't see my relief, I plunge ahead: "Do you know where she is, Sister?"

She picks up the beads of her dangling rosary and begins to draw them through her fingers.

"Her family has returned to Albany. I don't think Mr. Renard was happy here in his job at the comb shop and went back to his old one . . ."

"Nicole, was she glad to go back, too?" I ask. Then, conscious that I am pressing: "Do you think it might be all right if I visit her?"

She sighs, her shoulders lifting and falling, the beads clicking together as her fingers move across them.

"I don't know, Francis. She didn't seem happy when she came to say goodbye. Was she unhappy because she was leaving Frenchtown? Or was there something else? Did you quarrel, like young people do?"

Now it's my turn to sigh. If she asks that kind of question then she certainly doesn't know what happened with Larry LaSalle that night at the Wreck Center.

"Maybe it would be good to have a friend from Frenchtown visit her. It's hard for a young person like Nicole to move away from her friends . . ."

"Do you have her address, Sister?"

"She wrote me a letter a few weeks ago. She's in her senior year now, at St. Anne's. An academy of the Sisters of the Holy Spirit. I have her address upstairs in my bureau."

A few minutes later, we stand at the front door, our fingers touching tentatively as we shake hands. I have never touched a nun's flesh before. She lets go of my hand and touches the bandage on my face.

"I hope your face heals soon, Francis."

"A doctor I met in the service is going to help me. He's a specialist. I'll be as good as new pretty soon."

I wonder if it's a special sin to lie to a nun.

A moment later, I leave Sister Mathilde and the convent behind, Nicole Renard's address in my pocket.

For one lightning moment, I don't recognize her, fail to see Nicole Renard in the girl who has just entered the room. The long black hair that fell to her shoulders is gone. Now her hair is cut short and combed straight and flat, with wisps touching her ears. Her cheekbones are more prominent and her eyes seem to be bigger. I look at her as if studying a painting in a museum, searching for that glimpse of mischief in her eyes, but see only the question there.

"Francis," I announce, the way I did with Larry LaSalle and Sister Mathilde. "Francis Cassavant . . ."

She's wearing a green cardigan, unbuttoned, a white blouse underneath and a green plaid skirt, the uniform of the school. I saw other students dressed the same way when I entered the academy ground earlier this afternoon.

As she advances toward me, her face is inscrutable, and I wonder if my coming is a mistake, whether I should have written to her first. Instead, I took the train from Monument to Worcester, then to Albany, and a taxi to St. Anne's Academy. I convinced the nun at a desk in the administration building that I was harmless—a wounded veteran and a school friend of Nicole Renard's from Monument—and she ushered me, finally, into this parlor of plain furniture, paintings of saints on the paneled walls and an old classroom clock whose hands are frozen at six-thirty.

"I couldn't imagine who my visitor was," Nicole says, walking past me to the floor-to-ceiling glass door that looks out over a tennis court and green fields beyond. Maybe it was foolish of me to think that we would hug or even shake hands. "You've come a long way," she says.

"So have you."

She frowns and her eyes show concern. "How are you, Francis? Your face . . ."

"This is nothing," I say, gesturing toward the bandage and the scarf. "It's not as bad as it looks. My skin is healing. There's a doctor who took care of me overseas. He's going to fix my face up—they call it cosmetic surgery—when he gets back from the service." Still lying, but this time not to a nun.

"I heard about your Silver Star. Jumping on that grenade and saving all those lives. Remember Marie LaCroix? She writes me now and then, sends me news about Frenchtown."

"How about you, Nicole? How are you doing?" I don't want to talk about that grenade.

"Fine," she says, but the softness is gone from her face and her voice is sharp and brittle. "The girls here are very nice. Nuns are nuns, of course, but at least they don't use rulers for discipline here. So I'm fine."

You don't sound fine.

"I'm sorry about one thing," she says. "What I did to you that day."

"Did to *me*?" *What day?*

"I shouldn't have said those things to you that day on the piazza. You weren't to blame for what happened. I realized that later and went to your uncle Louis' place but found out that you'd enlisted."

We fall silent and she returns to the window, looking out as if something very interesting is going on out there. I join her and watch two girls in white blouses and shorts playing tennis. The ball when it lands doesn't have the sharp sound of a Ping-Pong ball on a table. Or a gunshot.

"He's dead, you know." It's easy to say the words because I'm not looking at her.

"I know."

"He was . . ."

"Don't say it, Francis. I know what he was. For a while there he made me feel special. Made us all feel special. Made me think I was a ballerina. Now I'm starting to find out what I am, who I really am . . ."

"Who are you, Nicole?"

"I told you—I'm just finding out." As if impatient with the question. Then: "How about you, Francis? How are you? What are you going to do now that you're back?"

I had prepared my answer while riding on the train. "Go to high school. College later. The GI Bill pays for college for veterans." The words sound flat and false to my ears.

"Are you going to write? I always thought you'd be a writer."

"I don't know." Which is the truth, for a change.

Silence falls between us, broken only by the

swish of the tennis racket and the plopping of the ball outside and the distant laughter of a girl in a corridor somewhere.

"Why did you come here today?" she asks.

The question surprises me. Didn't she know I'd track her down sooner or later?

"I wanted to see you again. To tell you that I'm sorry, too, for what happened. To see if . . ."

"If I was all right? To see if I had survived?" That bitter twist back in her voice again.

To see if maybe you could still be my girl. Which could maybe change my mind about the gun in my duffel bag.

"Well, I'm all right." Lifts her hands, palms upward. "What you see is what you get." A brave smile on her lips.

For once in my life, I'm not timid with her.

"I don't think so, Nicole."

"Don't think what?"

"I don't think you're all right."

She looks at me for a long moment, as still as the stopped clock on the wall.

"Did you ever tell anyone about it, Nicole? Did you ever talk about it?"

My question seems to startle her. "Who was I going to tell? My mother and father? It would have killed them, ruined them forever. Or maybe my father would have killed him, which would have been worse. The police? He was a big war hero. He didn't beat me up. No visible wounds. So I didn't tell anybody. All I said to my parents was that I didn't want to live in Frenchtown anymore. My father was ready to come back here, anyway. This is his hometown. And we came. No questions asked. I think they were afraid to ask questions."

She backs away, as if she needs to distance herself from me.

"Okay," she says. "If I'm not exactly all right, then I'm . . ." She screws up her face, searching for the right word. "I'm adjusting. Getting better at it all the time. When Marie LaCroix started writing to me, that Monument postmark gave me the shivers. I tore up that first letter. But she persisted. Now I read them and even write back." She sighs as if suddenly out of breath. "It's almost three years, Francis, and sometimes I can think of Frenchtown without the shivers. And then . . ." Her voice falters and her eyes lower.

"And then I come walking in."

She shakes her head. "For a minute there, when you said your name, I almost panicked. And I'm sorry. Because you were part of the good times, Francis. Always so shy, I couldn't help teasing you. Those movie matinees. Our long talks walking home." Reminiscence gentles her voice.

So we talk about those days and she confesses

that she really didn't like those cowboy serials and their fake endings every week but pretended to for my sake and I tell her that I was embarrassed that my palm was always wet when we held hands and she says her palm was wet, too. She says that Marie LaCroix was thinking of becoming a nun, which should liven up any convent. She tells me about the routine at St. Anne's. That she wants to be a teacher, English maybe. She asks me about the war and I keep it light, telling her the harmless things, about the crowded troopship going across and how the quality of sunlight in France is different somehow than in America.

We run out of words. Silence falls between us, magnifying the sounds of the tennis game outside, the plopping of the ball.

Finally, she reaches toward me.

"Your poor face," she says, moving as if to touch the white scarf, but I step away.

"I don't want you to see me this way," I tell her. "When the doctor fixes up my face, I'll send you a picture."

"Promise?"

"Promise," I answer, although I know that I will never keep that promise and that she probably doesn't expect me to.

She looks at me with affection. But affection is

not love. I've known all the time we've been talking that we're filling up the empty spaces between us with words. I've known that I've lost her, lost her a long time ago.

"I've got to go," I say. My gift to her.

She nods almost eagerly, glances at her watch. "The bell's going to ring any minute now. We live by bells around here."

She comes to me and doesn't reach for my face this time but takes my hand.

"Still moist," she says, tenderness in her voice. "My good Francis. My table tennis champion. My Silver Star hero . . ."

Hero. The word hangs in the air.

"I don't know what a hero is anymore, Nicole." I think of Larry LaSalle and his Silver Star. And my own Silver Star, for an act of cowardice.

"Write about it, Francis. Maybe you can find the answer that way."

"Do you think I can?"

"Of course you can." A trace of impatience in her voice. Like the Nicole Renard I knew at the Wreck Center just before the table tennis competition, urging me on. Telling me I could win.

She steps away. "Look, I've got to go." Suddenly brisk and hurried.

"Can I come again sometime?" I ask, hating myself for asking because I know the answer. It's as inevitable as the answer to an arithmetic problem Sister Mathilde wrote on the blackboard.

"Oh, Francis," she says, the words weighted with sadness. And I see the answer in her eyes.

She reaches up and presses her lips against the damp scarf that covers my own lips. I expect a flash of pain but there is only the pressure of her lips, and I close my eyes, clinging to the moment, wanting it to last forever.

"Have a good life, Francis. Be whatever will make you happy."

The bell rings, freezing us together for a moment, and when I open my eyes she is gone, the room vacant, her footsteps echoing down the hallway, until there's only silence left.

In the railroad station, sitting on the hard bench, I watch the people coming and going in the late-afternoon rush, on their way somewhere, with suit-cases and briefcases, a freckle-faced girl struggling under a knapsack on her back, two sailors sitting on the marble floor playing cards.

A master sergeant marches across the lobby as if leading an invisible platoon, uniform crisp, an array of ribbons on his chest. A young guy watches him, unshaven, wearing an old battle jacket, soiled and stained. He follows the sergeant with half-closed eyes, then sags against the wall, smiling dreamily. But the smile turns into a grimace and I wonder what he's thinking of or remembering.

I remember what I said to Nicole about not knowing who the real heroes are and I think of my old platoon. Sonny Orlandi, Spooks Reilly and Blinky Chambers. Eddie Richards and his diarrhea. Erwin Eisenberg. Henry Johnson, hit by shrapnel. And those who died, Jack Smith and Billy O'Brien, and all the others. I think of Enrico, minus his legs, his arm. I think of Arthur Rivier, drunk and mournful that night in the alley. *We were only there.* Scared kids, not born to fight and kill. Who were not only there but who stayed, did not run away, fought the good war. And never talk about it. And didn't receive a Silver Star. But heroes, anyway. The real heroes.

Maybe if I'm going to write as Nicole hopes I will, I should write about them.

Maybe I should buy a typewriter and get started.

Maybe I should try to find Dr. Abrams' telephone number in Kansas City.

Maybe I should track down Enrico, check out those hospitals he told me about.

I should do all those things.

I think of Nicole.

I think of the gun inside the duffel bag at my feet.

I pick up the duffel bag and sling it over my shoulder. The weight is nice and comfortable on my back as I cross the lobby, heading for the exit and the next train to leave the station.

ROBERT CORMIER has been called "the single most important writer in the whole history of young adult literature." His many acclaimed books include *The Chocolate War, I Am the Cheese, After the First Death, Beyond the Chocolate War, Fade, The Bumblebee Flies Anyway, We All Fall Down, Tunes for Bears to Dance To, In the Middle of the Night, Other Bells for Us to Ring, Eight Plus One, Tenderness, Heroes, Frenchtown Summer* and *The Rag and Bone Shop.* His books have won many awards and have been translated into several languages, becoming modern classics. In 1991 he received the Margaret A. Edwards Award, honoring his lifetime contribution to writing for teens.